THE DESPAIN PAPERS

THE DESPAIN PAPERS

by

George Sims

Dales Large Print Books
Long Preston, North Yorkshire,
England.

British Library Cataloguing in Publication Data.

Sims, George
    The Despain papers.

    A catalogue record for this book is
    available from the British Library

    ISBN 1-85389-697-7 pbk

Dales Large Print is an imprint of
Library Magna Books Ltd.
Printed and bound in Great Britain by
T.J. Press (Padstow) Ltd., Cornwall, PL28 8RW.

To
Jessica

'A man haunted by a fixed idea is insane.'
Conrad—NOSTROMO

CHAPTER 1

Friday night, September 25th, 1987

'Brief lives, brief lives.' The phrase echoed in Jack Quinn's mind in an irritating fashion. Irritating because he could hear it so clearly in a distinctive, feminine voice, but could not find a face to go with the voice. He seemed to remember a woman whispering the mocking comment in his ear about a group of people enjoying themselves, possibly at a party. He agreed that human existence was brief but could not understand why any human being should comment on the brevity in a scathing fashion.

Quinn felt dizzy and the room began to whirl round while the floor beneath his bed tilted ominously. He remembered that distant epoch when boxing was his favourite pastime and he had to come back into the ring feeling muzzy, even slightly unreal, with balls of cotton-wool pushed up into his nostrils and the taste

11

of bloody mucous leaking into his throat. Quinn knew it was night and knew that he was in a hospital, but that was the sum of his knowledge. Whatever had led up to his being in a hospital ward was a total blank. When he sent mental directions into his limbs they moved obediently, but these small exertions wearied him and when he tried to raise his head it made him dizzier. The young nurses padding about had cheerful, rallying voices for some of the other patients, but when he tried to question one of them she refused his enquiry by shaking her head firmly and then pantomimed going to sleep by folding her hands together to rest her head and slowly closing her eyes.

Had he been in a fight and taken so much punishment that he was punch drunk? He remembered two friends from the past, 'Fuzzy' Malone and 'What round is it?' Wynant, their faces maps of lost battles, with broken noses, balloons of scar tissue about their eyes and cauliflower ears. They had both reached the punch drunk stage of not knowing what was going on while still possessing the courage to continue fighting. Quinn patted his face to discover any injuries but the only area of pain, and that not severe, was a part of his right temple covered with a sticking plaster.

As he lay in the darkened ward searching for clues to his present predicament, vague memories came into his mind. What was real? Had he really seen a man's face which disturbed, even frightened him? Had he really been driven in an ambulance with someone complaining, 'all covered in blood, piss and snot'? Had a large, much distorted face hovered over him while a cut-throat razor was brandished before his eyes and a disembodied voice explained, 'Mr Quinn, Mr Quinn, we're just going to shave four small patches of your chest hair'? He dismissed the last memory as pure Hitchcock, too theatrical to be true, but when he fingered his chest there were indeed four small, bare patches. And had he been swearing, a monotonous stream of four-letter oaths, until he was reproved by a nurse? Quinn brooded on these dubious episodes while planning his escape from hospital. Nothing to it, he thought, they can't stop you discharging yourself when all that is wrong is a cut on the forehead.

Quinn had a strong antipathy towards

13

hospitals. This was not based on first-hand experience because he had only been in one for treatment, and that was just for a short period when he had an operation on his nose. His dread of such places, extending to all the smells, the humdrum routine, the tedium of waiting and the reduction of death to an everyday, run-of-the-mill matter, was based on the period when he had visited his father who was dying, seeing him grow weaker and more ill on each occasion. The old man had been brave and patient, and never complained, and his last words had been, 'Don't worry about me. I've had a happy life.' It was on that last visit that Quinn had decided he would much prefer to die on his own in the open air, far from doctors, nurses, hospitals and Intensive Care units, or hidden away like a cat.

Life in hospital, he thought, equalled life at second-hand, and a good deal of it was the life of an eavesdropper. As if to underline the point, at that moment he overheard part of a quiet conversation between two nurses:

'It's a black day for Mr Webster.'
'It's a downright inky day for Mr—.'

14

He did not catch the name of the man for whom the day would be inky, but he did hear one of the girls say in an amused tone 'And big with it.' There was some muted giggling after this comment.

Quinn said, 'Nurse, can I see whoever is in charge here?'

One of the nurses hurried over to his bedside. 'What, still awake? That's not right. You should be sleeping.'

'I'm wide awake and I want to see someone in charge. I don't know why I was brought in here but I feel okay now. I want to discharge myself and go.'

'No, you can't do that, Mr Quinn.'

'Well then let me talk to someone who can explain why I can't. What's wrong with me apart from being hungover and having a bang on the forehead?'

'I can't tell you that. You'll have to wait till morning and ask the staff nurse or sister if you can see Dr McGovern. You can do that after breakfast.'

'How do you know my name is Quinn? Did I talk to the doctor or somebody when I was brought in here?'

'I don't think you could talk much then. I think they found your name and address on some cards in your wallet. But you mustn't keep on talking to me. You'll tire yourself out, and I shall be in trouble too. Now, just try to go to sleep.'

When the nurse walked off Quinn felt so restive that he doubted his ability to become comfortable in the narrow bed, let alone sleep. He twisted about so much that he nearly fell out and suddenly laughed to himself, remembering some favourite lines by A A Milne he had often read to his daughters when they were small:

Our Teddy Bear is short and fat;
Which is not to be wondered at;
He gets what exercise he can
By falling off the ottoman...

When he managed to settle himself in the bed, Quinn reflected that what he had told the nurse was nowhere near the truth. He had become so used to bending the truth or lying by omission, in business and what he considered Romance, that he tended to do it automatically. If he had not been ill for several weeks, he certainly had been far from well. An unfortunate combination of viral 'flu, two series of antibiotics while taking other tablets for sinus trouble, not taking his blood pressure pills, the trauma of leaving Madeleine and his daughters, rushing to finish various jobs while he did not feel at all like working, this and that. A doctor might consider the biggest factor to be the dropping of his blood pressure tablets, particularly if he learnt it had not been done on medical advice, but Quinn felt that what had really laid him low was the conviction that he had made a terrible and probably irrevocable mistake in walking out of the marital home. He had done it impulsively, as he did most things, after an awful row with Madeleine in which bitter, wounding things had been said on both sides. A week after leaving Barton Street he would have done anything to put back the clock and still be living with his wife and the girls, even though the marriage had become a kind of truce and a matter of convenience, with little love on either side.

An older nurse bustled up to his bed, holding a glass of water and a tablet. 'Now you have this, Mr Quinn. It will help you sleep.'

Quinn protested that he thought he had been given some tablets already.

'Yes, we know exactly what you've had,

17

but nothing to help you sleep, and that is what you need now.'

While he swallowed the tablet, winning an approving nod from the nurse with grey hair, Quinn was thinking that usually he was immune to advice, particularly to anything that sounded like an order. His old man, Harry Joseph Quinn, had always been too easy on him, spoiling him, and subsequently he had very little experience of discipline. He had never been in the services and even his experience of working for someone else was limited. 'You always have a reason for doing something regardless of its effect. You only think about yourself,' Madeleine once said bitterly, and in a moment of unusual candour he acknowledged that this was true. He was fond of trotting out Oscar Wilde's quip, 'I can resist anything except temptation', and had come to believe that he could get away with it. Madeleine had proved that was not so.

After the older nurse had disappeared Quinn lay completely still, willing himself to sleep, but he could not help hearing another conversation between two young nurses: someone, it seemed, was in a bad way; someone was on tenorminls, atenol tablets, trintizal, largachl. Once more Quinn became agitated and restless. It was as if, somewhere in his head, a clock was ticking faster and faster, a relentless sound. Then in his mind's eye he suddenly saw his old friend Charlie Saunders gulping a dry digitalis tablet and swallowing water like an afterthought. He called out 'Charlie!' in a loud warning voice and swung both legs out of bed so that his feet touched the cold, highly polished linoleum.

'Mr Quinn! You're being very naughty! Back to bed! Sharp's the word! If you need something just ask us. That's what we're here for.' The older nurses's tone became less severe. 'Do try to settle down, Mr Quinn. That will help you...' She left the sentence unfinished but moved her head significantly towards the ward door, implying that sleep would help him in his desire to discharge himself from hospital.

Quinn nodded like an obedient child and said, 'Yes, thanks. Goodnight.' He lay back and closed his eyes though still troubled by strange memories, some of which he thought were counterfeit. His last thought was that he was in a maze without any idea how to escape.

CHAPTER 2

When Jack Quinn stared into the washroom mirror his father, Harry Joseph Quinn, seemed to peer out. Quinn knew that he was growing to look like his old man, but the similarity was more marked in the candid hospital mirror. In fact, from one angle, under the strip lighting, the similarity was striking. But there was a vital difference of expression. Harry Quinn had been a mild easy-going man, looking out calmly on a world he trusted. Jack Quinn's expression was cagey, as if he expected to be tricked or let down. 'O ye of little faith', Madeleine had said to him during one of their numerous rows and he had to acknowledge that there was some truth in it, as in most of her criticisms. Lack of faith in others and a strong sense of independence based on pride were the main reasons why Quinn hated the thought of ending up in hospital, completely dependent on others. 'You're always looking for the easy way out' was

20

another of Madeleine's little gibes which resounded in his brain as he washed, splashing his face with cold water in the hope of bringing some colour into his pale cheeks. Ginger stubble on his pointed chin gave him a somewhat villainous look, but he hoped that he did not look ill even though a queasy stomach had made him refuse the hospital breakfast.

'Mr Quinn? Finished?' Quinn recognized the nervous voice of the older nurse outside the washroom. When he opened the door she smiled and nodded vigorously. 'Yes, it's all right. Dr McGovern *will* see you this morning. Right now if you're ready.' She spoke with awe as if he had been granted an interview with the Queen. 'This way.' As he followed her along the corridor Quinn was occupied in thinking how he might best be able to give the impression of good health. He also reminded himself that there were two things he must not mention to McGovern: he must avoid saying anything that hinted at a loss of memory over the events of the previous evening for that would point to concussion, the need for X-rays and God knows what. And he must not say that he had given up taking his blood pressure tablets because he had read they could cause impotence.

When the grey-haired nurse knocked on a door there was an instant response of a deep voice saying, 'Come.' The nurse nodded again and urged Quinn forward.

'Dr McGovern? I'm Jack Quinn.'

The doctor was seated behind a large desk. He had iron-grey hair in such crimped waves that it looked as if he had been given a cheap perm. A pepper-and-salt moustache obscured his mouth. His grey eyes regarded Quinn with a less friendly look than he had expected.

'Ah yes, Mr Quinn. The gentleman who wishes to discharge himself.' He uttered the second sentence as if it were a joke.

'I can discharge myself, can't I?'

'You can indeed but you should ask yourself if it's wise. Sit down Mr Quinn.' The doctor indicated a small chair facing his large one.

There was a pause during which the doctor scrutinised him closely. When McGovern did speak, his Edinburgh Morningside accent was noticeable and he had the tone of someone much put upon.

'Mr Quinn, now tell me, just how do you think you got here last night? Do you imagine that you simply walked into reception complaining of a small gash to your forehead and we rushed you into Casualty?'

The doctor's raised eyebrows, his unfriendly expression and the rhetorical question made Quinn think that the interview was not going to be as easy as he had expected.

'No, I'll tell you how you came to be here, and the state you were in.' McGovern picked up a small piece of paper. 'Last evening you must have had far too much to drink, enough to make you quite incoherent. And it appears you also became grossly over-excited, about what we do not know. You fell down, striking your head against a telephone-box. Fortunately you were spotted by a police constable. This PC Wheatley went to your assistance and was perceptive enough to realise you weren't just a drunk making an ass of yourself. He flagged down an ambulance that was passing and you arrived here half-conscious on a stretcher, using the most foul language. The one thing that did make sense was your confession to the nurse that you had stopped taking your blood pressure tablets. So you entered our casualty ward drunk, over-excited and with a blood pressure reading of 220 over 130! A fatal combination. I mean, it could have been fatal. You could have gone like that!' McGovern snapped his fingers decisively.

'I'm sorry about the swearing. I'll apologise...'

McGovern waved this away. 'It's not important. Nurses take things like that in their stride. What is important is stopping your Navidrex-K. Why did you do that?'

'I had an attack of viral 'flu and my doctor prescribed antibiotics, and I was already taking other tablets for sinus. My nose was broken and the operation on it didn't work...'

'But what has all that to do with your blood pressure tablets?'

'I thought I was taking too many tablets.'

'By God man, you mustn't make those kind of decisions! Always ask your doctor about things like that!'

'Yes, I can see that now. I was stupid.'

The admission seemed to mollify the doctor, who ran a hand over his corrugated hair while staring again at the piece of paper. He asked, 'You're married, Mr Quinn?'

'Yes.'

'And you live at, ah I see, Bourdon Street. Well, you should be comfortable enough there. I have no objection to you leaving us as long as you behave sensibly; have a couple of days in bed, let your wife make a fuss of you, and keep taking the tablets we prescribe. Then go and see your doctor. In fact, if you're ready in half an hour I can drop you off at the corner. It's on my way home.'

CHAPTER 3

Tommy laughed at one of Tom's sly jokes as they hurried through the Burlington Arcade. She had an infectious, silvery laugh and people turned on hearing it, then continued to stare because Tom and Tommy were an exceptionally attractive couple. Tom was exactly six feet tall and Tommy was only four inches shorter. They were slim as well as tall, and they both had blonde hair, tanned complexions and very white teeth. Tom's hair appeared a little darker than Tommy's but this was due to it being greased straight back in the style of a 1930s film star. It was their eyes that often led strangers into thinking that they must be twins: large eyes of a sea-green colour with dark lashes. Tom was the more unusual looking of the pair—a hint of effeminacy in his sensual lips and long-lashed eyes was effectively dispelled by his prognathous chin and the wolfish effect of his smile since his mouth seemed to contain too many teeth, though all of them were straight due to some orthodontic trickery.

Momentarily frustrated by the unmoving crowd who appeared hypnotised by the expensive goods on offer in the arcade, Tom muttered Dostoevsky's phrase, 'poor, suffering humanity' but he said it in a contemptuous way which negated the Russian novelist's intention. Tommy grinned and used her sharp elbows to make a path, tugging at Tom's wrist. When the couple looked at each other it was plain that if they were indeed twins their relationship must be an incestuous one.

Marching along briskly, without a glance at the windows full of jewellery, silverware and cashmere garments, Tom and Tommy appeared to be living in a world of their own. They both needed to socialise for business reasons, and Tom had a passion for gambling which Tommy did not share, but they always returned to each other with relief. Alone in a rented flat or a hotel bedroom, they were like animals with a great hunger to assuage. When they were by themselves they used a private language with key phrases such as 'a cruel 'oax', and references to the odd world created by Beatrix Potter, often re-christening new acquaintances with the names of her characters such as 'Jeremy Fisher', 'Hunca Munca' and 'Samuel Whiskers'. Occasionally, when it was pertinent, Tom would allude to himself as 'Mr Tod', probably the most ruthless animal in the Beatrix Potter menagerie.

When they emerged from the Piccadilly entrance to the arcade they walked along in the direction of Piccadilly Circus, then stopped to look up at the famous clock on the eau-de-nil facade of Fortnum & Mason, the clock which is supported by two pavilions cast in solid bronze. Standing close together, silent and unmoving, the handsome couple looked unreal, like models in a shop window, or emissaries from another planet, staring out at the world with unusually large eyes.

'Is Mr McGregor still a problem?' Tommy asked Tom, using the Beatrix Potter name they had given to a painstaking and persistent CID man, Detective Inspector Jimmy Ross, who had been closing in on the dashing duo, unaware that Tom might become 'Mr Tod' and use his cut-throat razor if he felt threatened.

'Yes, Mrs Puddleduck. I think I shall have to make some permanent arrangement concerning Mr McGregor.'

Tommy did not reply to this statement but a shadow seemed to pass over her face. She put on a pair of sunglasses with dark blue lenses. After a minute or two she asked 'And what about Tommy Brock?', using their private sobriquet for Franceso Manservigi, the proprietor of a gambling club to whom Tom owed a vast sum. Tom shrugged and pulled a funny face which conveyed to Tommy that he was tired of questions.

Though it was not yet nine o'clock on a Saturday morning, Piccadilly swarmed with people, many of them tourists. A crowd began to form about the couple, staring up, like them, at the bronze pavilions. Tom opened his clenched right hand to disclose his Roman coin which he always carried as a lucky piece. He claimed that it was his sole inheritance from his father. 'Dear chum, this is my wager' he said quietly and held it in his left hand high above his head. Tommy was not altogether surprised that he should choose his favourite possession. I'll match you, she thought, easing off the ancient Osiris ring he had given her in Cairo when they first met. 'And this is mine' she said, handing over the ring to him with a smile. Tom gave her one of his rare kind of smiles which acknowledged a show of spirit, and held the ring up in his right hand.

Tommy noticed some admiring glances from women standing about them, directed at Tom. She was amused to think of the illusions they would have about him, looking as if he had not a care in the world, immaculately dressed in a grey flannel suit, white cotton shirt and a Sulka silk tie of black and white diamonds. She thought how amazed the women would be if they knew that she and Tom were adventurers, 'two against the world', who believed that human existence was a bad joke or a 'cruel 'oax' as it had once been described to her by a Berkshire countryman. Adventurers living on their wits, taking as their motto the quotation: 'living well is the best revenge'.

At nine o'clock the hinged doors on the two pavilions opened and through them appeared the figures of Mr Fortnum and Mr Mason, each about four feet high, in eighteenth century costume. As the clock commenced to chime the figures moved forward to the edge of their respective platforms, then turned inwards and bowed to each other. When the clock stopped chiming, the tune 'The Lass with the Delicate Air' was played on bells.

Tommy's eyes were concentrated on the performance of Mr Fortnum and Mr Mason, but her mind was elsewhere, thinking that she and Tom were in a dangerous position *vis a vis* Francesco Manservigi whom Tom had once described as 'a long-nosed, wholly predatory animal'. Still, she mused, no matter how desperate their situation she could not have a better partner than someone who did not know what fear was. She thought of a similarly dangerous occasion when they had been in confrontation with a powerful Tong leader in New York. The perilous encounter had taken place in a tiny delicatessen in Canal

Street which formed a kind of border-line between New York's Little Italy and Chinatown. They had been surrounded by Mr Quong's threatening minions but once again the devil-may-care Tom had triumphed.

Mr Fortnum and Mr Mason bowed to each other again, turned about and moved back into their pavilions. Tom asked Tommy 'Did they bow again?' but his question was rhetorical. When she nodded he gave her a wry look and said, 'So, then, you lose, Mrs Puddleduck.' With just a small movement of his right arm he threw the Osiris ring high into the air so that it disappeared a hundred feet away among the slow-moving traffic.

CHAPTER 4

By the time McGovern's Jaguar XJS stopped at the corner of Davies Street and Bourdon Street the doctor knew quite a lot about Quinn, but it included some misinformation because Quinn kept up the pretence that he had a wife at home who would be glad to look after him. On the other hand McGovern divulged nothing about himself except that he enjoyed watching boxing on television. He appeared interested to hear that Quinn was a dealer in rare books, with an office in Davies Street, and expressed disappointment that the stock did not include any old books on medicine.

While Quinn was fiddling with his seat-belt McGovern said, 'That nose operation to straighten the septum...Mind, I don't want to be quoted on this...sub-mucus resections are often unsatisfactory because a number of patients have adhesions or some other kind of trouble. Go back to your surgeon and tell him you are not satisfied. You don't want a lifetime of sinus trouble. And the type of tablets you are dosing yourself with don't mix well with alcohol!'

Quinn got out of the Jaguar, thanking the doctor for his advice but without any intention of taking it. Before he closed the car door McGovern held him with another question—'Tell me, do you have one of those old merchants' houses, with the pulley-like attachment at the end of the gable?'

'Yes, I do, that one with the dark blue door.'

'Very attractive—and what a situation! Tucked away and quiet yet only two minutes from New Bond Street.'

'Yes, but I only have it for two years. I bought the tail end of a long lease...' Quinn stopped, realising that he was using the word 'I' when he should be saying 'We' to include a loving wife.

McGovern said goodbye, pointing at Quinn as he added, 'Now, remember—at least two days' rest!'

Quinn waved and turned on his heel to walk down Bourdon Street, thinking how ironic his situation was. For years he had fancied the old houses in Bourdon Street, not a hundred yards from his office, but now that he had one it seemed dust and ashes. It was a strange coincidence that he had heard of the lease being for sale just when his rows with Madeleine had reached the worst point ever. He had boasted that he could easily move out and she had called his bluff: the next evening, when he returned to the Barton Street house which her father had bought for them, he found all his belongings neatly packed in cartons and cases. Madeleine's scrupulous fairness in selecting his records and books, the fact that she put on his piles any over which there might have been an argument, showed that she welcomed the chance to be rid of him.

Before putting his key into the lock Quinn glanced at his watch and swore when he saw that it was half-past eleven. His daughters had formed the habit of calling in at his bachelor establishment at about nine o'clock on Saturday mornings, but they would not have waited two hours for him to turn up. Ascending the blue-carpeted stairs, he was sure that Liz and Dolly had been there for the carpet had been swept more efficiently than he had ever managed it. From their mother the girls had inherited good looks, charm, social manners and a passion for neatness. He was glad about that but also pleased that from him they had a love of nature, music and books.

Going into the bathroom he saw that the good fairies had been there too, putting the top back on the tube of toothpaste, cleaning the bath and replacing the towels. He looked in the mirror at his stubbly cheeks but decided to leave shaving until after a nap; he felt weary and was going to take McGoverns' advice and spend most of the day in bed.

The kitchen had also been tidied and swept. Propped up against a nearly empty jar of instant coffee there was a letter in Liz's careful italic script:

Dearest Daddy, We were here. Where were you??!! Mr Strachey is taking us to Remenham this afternoon and we shall be staying the night there. Can you collect us tomorrow afternoon, about teatime? We hope so. Please phone Mrs Strachey and let her know, either way. If you or your old car are out of order we shall have to come back by train.

Lots of love, Liz

PS. Harpo the parrot is still not talking but he does good imitations of our whistling. Groucho the cat is fine.

Another postscript had been added in Dolly's scrawly handwriting which was much like his own:

Dearest Daddy, When are you going to buy a bookcase or have some book-shelves made? And some more furniture for the living room? You know that

Mummy would call it a disgraceful tip! Things you need to buy right away: Nescafé, toilet-rolls, washing-up liquid (get Fairy), box of tissues or kitchen roll towel (paper), toothpaste. We hope very much to see you and ye ancient Mercedes tomorrow.

Your loving Dolly

Reading the letters had a markedly beneficial effect on Quinn. It was plain that his daughters were still maintaining their neutral attitude towards him and their mother. They knew all his faults but did not seem to think he was wholly to blame for the separation. He looked forward to an afternoon and evening in their company. He might even look in at the Barton Street house when he took them home, and see if Madeleine was still so pleased to be rid of him.

Quinn started to undress in a piecemeal fashion by kicking off his shoes. Then he walked into the living-room while singing a song which had been handed down to him by his father and which his daughters also enjoyed:

I'm all airs and graces
I'm Burlington Bertie from Bow
Bert, Bert...
I haven't a shirt
But my people are well off
You know...

As he looked round the living-room Quinn had to admit that it was a bit of a tip. He had placed the unpacked cartons of books and records on the faded blue carpet inherited from the previous tenant. The only item of furniture in the room was a large couch which he had bought in Marylebone Lane. The cartons summed up a large part of his life. One was full of George Gershwin records, including several different versions of favourite tunes—'your Gershwin mania' as Madeleine had put it. There were also some very old 78s which belonged to his mother who had died when he was two years old, evidence of what Madeleine termed his obsession with the past. That she had no obsession for the past nor any nostalgia for it was evident when she placed the Beatles' record 'She loves you' on a pile for him to take, for it had been a great favourite of theirs when they first became lovers.

Another carton contained the books he had read to his daughters at various stages in their lives. There were no books in the flat over his father's antique shop in Hammersmith where Quinn grew up, so he had discovered the appeal of A A Milne, Kenneth Grahame and Lewis Carroll rather late in life and characters like Toad in *The Wind in the Willows* had become favourites with him just as they were with Dolly and Liz.

Quinn walked into his bedroom thinking that while it might be a bit under-furnished it did contain some of the world's greatest paintings. He was quite willing to admit to an obsession with Botticelli which had not been shared by Madeleine, so his three Botticelli reproductions had never graced the walls of the Barton Street house. Now his favourite, 'The Birth of Venus', was over his bed, the mysterious 'La Primavera' was on the facing wall so that it was the first thing he saw on waking, and the small exquisite 'Mars and Venus' was by the window.

He took off his jacket and trousers and placed them in the wardrobe. He was relieved to see that his car keys were nestling in a pullover placed on the chair, since that meant his old Mercedes had not been involved in the mysterious adventures of Friday evening.

Wearily Quinn lay down on the bed, pulling the pale blue duvet over him; he felt as if he could sleep for a week. But the moment his head touched the pillow he had the strange, fleeting impression that his oldest friend, Charlie Saunders, was involved in some danger with his BMW. Momentarily he felt like getting out of bed to warn Charlie although he had no idea how that could be accomplished. He concentrated his thoughts on his daughters—Liz playing the piano and looking just like her mother and Dolly trying to persuade Harpo, the African grey parrot, to talk. These peaceful images allowed him to relax and let go of consciousness.

CHAPTER 5

'Mr Tod' had 'Mr McGregor' under the closest observation. Tom's keen eyesight was quite adequate to watch Detective Inspector Ross's every move, but Tom observed Ross through expensive binoculars since he liked to note any quirk of behaviour and the slightest change of expression on Ross's face. Also a binocular view of things added to Tom's god-like feeling of being in charge of the fate of the one who was so closely scrutinised. 'Mr Tod' had an intent yet faintly amused expression as he watched 'Mr McGregor', and when he talked to himself it was in a quiet, jovial voice which 'Mrs Puddleduck' had never heard.

Tom's view of the universe was bleak indeed; he believed that man grappled with his personal destiny and inevitably lost, but he took every step he could to postpone the inevitable. He knew that Detective Inspector Jimmy Ross was a member of the élite SO11, formerly C11, the most secretive of Scotland Yard's departments, with its motto *sceleratus non scelus*, meaning concentrate on the criminal rather than the crime. SO11 specialised in the gathering of criminal intelligence, placing villains under surveillance and so enabling officers in other branches to arrest them red-handed. Tom took particular pleasure in placing a specialist in such matters under surveillance. He had made it his business to learn as much as possible about Ross and knew that the detective had the reputation of being a loner who played his cards close to his chest, so that it was likely that Ross had kept his day-to-day movements to himself. He also knew that Ross, though aged only forty, was a widower so there was no wife to hear any confidences about what he was doing. Ross lived alone in a flat in the Barbican, was a former rugby player, no mean athlete and something of a tough guy.

Tom was hopelessly addicted to gambling and he preferred to play when the stakes were more than he could afford to lose. He looked on 'coming to a permanent arrangement' with an enemy as the highest form of gambling, for in such an encounter both lives were inevitably at stake because the victim might have Chance on his side. Although Tom appeared calm as he waited and watched he was in fact intensely excited—nothing else in life gave him such a buzz as terminating another's existence. He found the sense of power quite intoxicating. Ross and Tom had one thing in common: courage. But Ross was an example of the rule that brave men lack imagination, while Tom was an exception to that rule in that he was fearless and yet had a sick imagination fashioned by events in his past.

The vantage point for watching 'Mr McGregor' was a seedy, partly furnished Thames-side house doomed to demolition when its short lease expired. Ross was standing on the corner of the empty street; it was a Sunday morning and hardly anyone was about. Ross leant against a wall and glanced at a newspaper from time to time. In the small bedroom where Tom waited there was a black briefcase and matching suitcase on the threadbare carpet. Tom looked incongruous in the shabby flat since he was immaculately dressed in a light grey flannel suit, white cotton shirt and black and white polka-dotted tie. He had added an appropriately funereal touch with a black display handkerchief. He felt that the moment of crisis in Ross's life was fast approaching because the detective had consulted his wristwatch twice in five minutes. 'If I read your mind right, Mr McGregor,' Tom said quietly, 'and I usually do. You see, it's a hobby of mine. If I read your mind right, then Sunday's the day you make your move and inspect these old premises.' He paused for a moment and added, 'Remember that life's just a cabaret, old chum. Come to the cabaret!'

Tom scrutinised Ross's face once more and then put down the binoculars and took some rubber gloves from the black briefcase. He took off his jacket and placed it over the back of a wooden chair. When he pulled on the gloves he looked like a surgeon relishing getting to grips with a tricky operation. As he walked quietly down the bare wooden stairs towards the front door he smiled to himself at the thought that Detective Inspector Ross had the greatest surprise of his life coming to him. He stood where he would be hidden when the front door was opened and picked up a grimy brick he had placed on the doormat. He stood motionless, straining to hear any sound from the road outside. He would have staked all that he and Tommy possessed on a bet that Ross would try to enter the terrace house within five minutes. He opened his mouth and sang, quite soundlessly, 'Life is a cabaret, old chum. Only a cabaret, old chum. Come to the cabaret.' As he did so he lifted the brick up and down in his gloved left hand. 'Come on, come on, come on!' he mouthed, and, as if in answer to his silent plea, heard the sound of quick footsteps coming towards the door and a key being inserted in the lock. Tom tensed himself for action, savouring the thought that it might possibly be a fatal move for himself. All was in the balance. As always there was pleasure in skirting disaster.

The door opened slowly and Ross took a cautious, fatal step as Tom swung the brick with just enough force to stun the detective who collapsed at the knees and fell face forward. Within seconds Tom had closed the front door and pocketed the key which had fallen from Ross's hand. A few more seconds and Tom was dragging the unconscious man up the stairs. The blow with the brick had been nicely judged so that Ross was not dripping blood.

Once the detective was in the front bedroom Tom set to work with a coil of washing line he took from the black briefcase. Like a spider wrapping up his prey, Tom started to wind the rope round Ross's ankles, having first laid a length of the line from his victim's ankles to his neck. He wound the rope very tightly and closely as if he was binding up a broken fishing-rod. When he had finished his work Ross's head appeared to be attached to a great bundle of rope. Tom finished off the parcel by tying the two ends of the line with a reef knot. He looked down at the result with satisfaction and said in his quiet, friendly 'Mr Tod' voice, 'Get out of that, Houdini, and you won't have to arrest me. I'll give myself up.' He dragged the bound body across the room and propped it up in the cupboard which had served as a wardrobe. He took some cotton-wool and a large sticking plaster from his briefcase, stuffed the wool into Ross's mouth and used the plaster to close it permanently. He locked the cupboard and pocketed the key, put the binoculars into the briefcase and donned his elegant jacket. As he removed the rubber gloves he looked round the room to see if anything had been left there. Picking up the two black cases, he walked down the stairs whistling 'Come to the cabaret'.

The detective's body would probably be found in six months' time when the house was due to be demolished, but Tom was not the sort of man who worried about possible events that were six months off.

CHAPTER 6

'Brief lives!' The phrase again returned to Jack Quinn's mind to irritate him, as he knew it would until he was able to match the voice with a face. It was a perfect autumn afternoon, so sunny and warm it seemed as if summer had returned. Quinn stood at an idyllic little spot within a stone's throw of the River Thames at Remenham. Upstream he could see the church tower and houses at Henley; downstream, the Chiltern hills. Quinn's fingers were entwined in the wire netting surrounding a hard tennis court and he was supposed to be watching his daughter Dolly playing tennis with her best friend Gillian Strachey. He kept thinking that he must concentrate on the game, for the girls had asked him to act as umpire in the case of any doubtful calls, but the slightest thing seemed to distract him. His eye was taken by the rapid swoop and glide of a seagull above the river, then he noticed a plump squirrel toying with something in its tiny hands. Quinn's mind was too full of memories and thoughts to do the job of umpire. Suddenly another memory of the mysterious female slotted into place and he could hear her saying, 'If I read your mind right, Mr Jeremy Fisher...' Why should the unknown woman have called him Jeremy Fisher, the name of the frog in one of Beatrix Potter's books? He mentally strained to think of an answer to this little puzzle but all his memory proffered him was the phrase 'Rich is best' in the same voice and with infectious, silvery laughter.

'Out!'

'In! It was definitely in.'

'Out. Miles out!'

'On the line. Daddy, it was on the line, wasn't it?'

Quinn recovered from tussling with intractable memories to say, 'Sorry, darling. Sorry, but I'm not sure.'

'Oh Daddy, that's pathetic! You *must* know. And you're supposed to have such wonderful eyesight. What a swiz!'

Dolly bent down to pick up a glossy conker from the green macadam surface of the court and hit it hard to express her indignation so that the horse-chestnut zoomed up and out of the court.

Gillian Strachey shouted decisively, 'So game, set and championship point! Miss Strachey the winner!' she put down her racquet on the court and executed a victor's jig around it, a delightful little dance that semed to Quinn to have all the spontaneity and grace of youth.

Quinn pointed to the graze on his forehead. 'Sorry, missis,' he said to Dolly. 'It was the bang on the head what did it. Lack of concentration, that is.'

'Just pathetic! I've been swindled,' said Dolly, walking up to the net to collect her dark blue cardigan which hung from the winding handle.

'Shouldn't you play the point again?' Quinn queried. 'As the point was doubtful.'

'No way,' said Gillian. 'Local rule, you see.'

Dolly laughed. 'You are an idiot, Jill. Local rule my eye.'

Gillian rushed up to Dolly and put her arm round her waist. 'Let's pack it in anyway and go for a walk. Do you want to come Jack? We'll go along to the lock and buy ice-creams.'

'Thanks, but I think I'll try to track Liz down. You said she went off in the direction of the church?'

'Yes, but she said she was going "botanising" so she could be anywhere.'

The two girls exchanged significant glances as they put on their cardigans before coming out from the court. Quinn wondered what these looks signified. He had an insatiable curiosity about what made people tick. This had led him into trouble at times, because some of his 'romances' had started by him simply being fascinated by what was going on in a woman's head; he loved the rare moments during pillow talk when a woman would confide secrets. The girls stood with their arms around each other's waist. They were both flushed by their exertions but on them it looked good. Gillian had honey-coloured hair and bright blue eyes but Quinn thought Dolly was the more attractive and felt free to come to this judgement since neither Dolly nor Liz looked at all like him.

'Well, if you're sure you're sure about the walk...' Dolly said. 'We're not in any great rush to go back to London, are we?'

Quinn shook his head. 'Not as far as I'm concerned. I'm in your hands, miss.'

'Right then, so we'll see you. Byeee.'

Quinn stood still for a few minutes after

the girls had set off on their walk along the river bank. He was savouring the afternoon, regretting that it would be finished all too soon, agreeing with the mysterious voice about life being brief. Yes, how short life is, how quickly things change, Quinn thought. He had the momentary impulse to write a poem with the title 'A child in the house', about the pleasure of having children around and the inevitable poignancy of the relationship as the children were always moving away by growing up.

Instead of walking up the lane to the church, Quinn was drawn to the edge of the Thames by the sight of a pair of swans sailing about sedulously as if under orders to be decorative. Quinn sighed and briefly envied Bill Strachey with his delightful riverside house and settled domestic life. What a fool I've been, he thought as he watched the majestic swans and a cloud of midges doing a weird kind of dance just above the surface of the river.

He sighed again and turned on his heel to cross the stile and walk up the lane. As he did so an answer, unsought, came into his mind and he was able to visualise the girl who had whispered 'Brief lives' to him. She was tall with blond hair, a Botticelli-like face and a mysterious smile. He also remembered a bright gaiety, perhaps a touch too much as if the gaiety masked a reined-in hysteria or some neurotic secret. He had been at a party and the blonde girl was by his side, looking across a large room, watching people in the slightly artificial atmosphere of such a gathering. The girl had noticed that his gaze was directed at another woman, a red-haired beauty with lovely, down-slanting eyes, and said, 'If I read your mind right, Mr Jeremy Fisher, I expect you think all her zones would be erogenous.'

Now, one more little matter, Quinn urged his recalcitrant memory—a name to go with the face that goes with the voice. No name came to mind though he could hear the girl's laugh and seemed to remember a tiny waist. That's quintessential Quinn he thought—no name is filed but the impression of a twenty-inch waist is duly recorded. He walked quickly up the lane which ran at the back of a barn, and then paused by the lych-gate to Remenham churchyard, hoping to glimpse Liz's green dress. He entered the gate, attracted by the sight of an elaborate

51

tomb with a seated female statue, but as he approached it his attention was taken by a pair of gravestones beneath a large yew tree. The old italic lettering on them had been cleaned of lichen to make every word distinct. The one on the left bore a touching poetical tribute:

To the Memory of
SARAH the wife of
Caleb Gould
Who died Oct 18 1813
Aged 69 years

Lo! where this silent stone now weeps
A Friend, A Wife, A Mother sleeps
A heart, within whose sacred cell
The peaceful virtues loved to dwell
Affection, warmth and faith sincere
And soft humanity were there

The stone on the right also bore a brief poem:

To the Memory of
CALEB GOULD
Who died May 30 1836
Aged 92 years

This world's a jest
And all things show it
I thought so once
But now I know it

Quinn brooded over the poem on Caleb Gould's gravestone, thinking: There's something wrong with it, something about the punctuation which is not the same as the epitaph that the poet John Gay had written for himself. Then he laughed at himself, for such a thought was also quintessential Quinn. It was the kind of thing he was apt to do in the catalogues of rare books he compiled—stress some fussy, pedantic point and overlook the salient feature. What did it matter if the punctuation on Caleb's stone wasn't the same as John Gay's? The important thing about the two stones was the contrast between the lyrical inscription to Sarah and the bitter, disillusioned lines old Caleb had chosen for himself some twenty-three years later. Although it was warm, Quinn shivered. He wasn't in the mood to brood on death and despair; what he wanted was to make the most of the brief time with his girls.

With a perfunctory glance at the tomb

with the seated female figure, Quinn walked back across the grassy graves to the lych-gate. The sky was completely blue apart from a few white clouds grouped together on the horizon to the west. It was the kind of weather he liked best but he wasn't really enjoying it, feeling low and tired. Hungry too—it was half-past five and all he had eaten was a bowl of muesli for breakfast and a Cox's Orange Pippin on the journey from London. Tea had not been offered by the Stracheys though he had expected it, and a cucumber sandwich would not have come amiss. He decided to stop somewhere on the way back to London and have supper with the girls even if it did mean they would be a bit late back at Barton Street.

As he walked back down the lane Quinn could hear the steady sound of Bill Strachey's motor-mower, and thought that perhaps tea would be on offer later in the Strachey household when the master had finished his garden chores. Within sight of a distant curve of the Thames he heard the exciting sound of swans flying and then saw them rise just above the level of the trees; he envied Bill Strachey again despite all the work that must be involved in keeping a large garden tidy. Crossing the stile he looked both ways along the tow-path, hoping to see a green dress or two girls in white tennis clothes, but they were nowhere in sight. He was drawn by the prospect of Henley as the sun sank down into clouds which imperceptibly changed shape and became larger; the sun gilded their edges and coloured them primrose, pink and gold until they resembled a mysterious landscape which could be reached by a few giant strides into the sky. As he stood still, enjoying the sunset, he was struck by the thought that there had been something very odd and dream-like about the party where the Botticelli-type girl had whispered into his ear.

'Daddy! Daddy! Jack!' Excited female shouts made him turn round, and he saw his daughters and Gillian Strachey running towards him. Liz's dress looked slightly old-fashioned but very attractive—it was just the sort of thing that Madeleine would choose.

Gillian said in a breathless voice, 'Jack, Mummy wants to know if you will all take pot luck and have an early supper here.'

Before Quinn could reply Dolly threw an arm round his waist, pleading, 'We can stay Daddy, can't we? Say we can.'

Quinn said, 'Grand! What a nice idea! The best offer I've had for days.'

Gillian looked at him in a detached, slightly critical fashion. 'Do you always wear dark blue shirts?'

Quinn nodded. 'I'm a terrible shopper.'

Dolly added, 'If Marks and Spencer don't stock it, forget it.'

Liz took Quinn's right arm, saying, 'He just asks an M & S girl to point him in the direction of dark blue shirts and grey tweed jackets.'

'Five minutes, in and out,' Dolly went on.

Gillian said confidentially, after a quick look about her, 'Daddy and I were wondering, Jack, if you could find us a first edition in nice condition of Mrs Beeton's Cook Book. As a birthday present for Mum. Have to be within the next month because her birthday's on the third of November.'

'Ah!' said Dolly. 'That's a different matter. When it comes to finding first editions, Dad's ace.'

Quinn said, 'Yes, leave it to me. That's a little job I shall enjoy. I'll have a word with Bill on the q.t.'

Walking back along the river path, with a loving daughter on each arm, Quinn thought: So what if life is a jest and it leads nowhere but the grave, it's still worth it for moments like this.

CHAPTER 7

Monday the 28th of September 1987 was a fine autumn day with mist slowly clearing to disclose a bright blue sky, but Jack Quinn was not in a good mood because the day had started badly for him. After a restless night of disturbed sleep and nonsenical dreams he had woken feeling as if he had not slept at all, and realised that he should have taken Dr McGovern's advice about having two days in bed.

It was ten minutes past nine when Quinn reached his office in Davies Street and found that there was no welcoming pile of post on June Whitall's desk but Cyril Parkinson was already on the premises, moving around June's office, which also served as a showroom, with tortoise-like slowness. Quinn strode through the room with a curt 'Hello' and a nod of recognition; June pulled a funny face to acknowledge his reactions to the absent post and the presence of C Parkinson.

Once inside his own office, with the door firmly closed behind him, Quinn went to the window and looked down Davies Street to Berkeley Square, a pleasant prospect in bright sunshine, and silently cursed the Post Office and Parkinson. He had looked forward to having some stimulating letters which would enable him to forget temporarily the mysterious events of Friday evening. He always took late deliveries of mail personally, as if the postmen were trying to sabotage his small business, though he knew that June was right to call this reaction 'paranoid'. Cyril Parkinson's presence was another source of irritation, for although the door was shut he could visualise Parkinson's agonisingly slow progress along the bookshelves, taking books down and holding them in his large, dry-looking hands as if he were weighing them. What was worse, he could imagine Parkinson's comments in his dry, pompous voice: 'John Galsworthy now. I suppose he's a very unfashionable author today. Can't be much call for his first editions I should think, yet you've priced *The Man of Property* at £150! Is he still collected at all I wonder...'

Quinn's door opened and June came through with a humorous look as if she knew exactly what he was thinking. She said, 'I see you've been in the wars again.'

Quinn touched the scab on his forehead in a brushing-off gesture. 'Nothing much. I walked into a door.' On a piece of typing paper he scribbled a note: 'Do you think Parkinson will be here long? I CAN'T STAND IT TODAY.' June wrote a neat reply with her customary underlining: 'Cyril Parkinson *buys* books. We are *supposed* to *sell* books. QED. No reason why *you* have to see him. SO WHY WORRY?'

In a loud voice, pitched so that Parkinson could probably hear her, June said, 'Just one phone call before you arrived. At nine o'clock precisely. From that nice Mr Eckstein. Must have been keen to contact us—surely it would be the middle of the night in New York? Anyway, he said that he'd posted us an express airmail packet last week and was surprised we hadn't received it...'

'He doesn't appreciate our erratic postal service...'

'So he said that when the packet does reach us will you kindly revise the offer he made in the enclosed letter as he is now prepared to pay three thousand five hundred pounds for the Gerald Despain papers—the complete collection that is. He also wanted me to say that he is very interested in buying the German part of the collection if Mr Principle does not want to sell the lot. Does that mean anything to you?'

Quinn had pencilled down the names Moishe Eckstein and Gerald Despain with a line joining them: he added the £3500 in very large letters and underlined it, saying, 'I know the name Gerald Despain all right. He was one of the British traitors who went to Germany in World War II, did some broadcasting for the Nazis like "Lord Haw-Haw", but he was mainly a journalist, writing Nazi propaganda, fanatical anti-Jewish stuff. But Principle, that's an unusual name—did you check it?'

'Yes, I did, I spelt it back in case he meant Principal.'

'You think of everything, Junie! This is

the one biz where the Girl Friday is just a shade more efficient than the Robinson Crusoe.'

'Flattery will get you most things. Shall I make some coffee?' She lowered her voice, 'I ought to make some for you know who.'

'Coffee will just about hit the spot. You're worth your weight in lapis lazuli.'

'Is that good or bad I ask myself. And I thought it was agreed between us that the subject of my weight should never be raised here.' June's shapely but plump figure disappeared out of the door and Quinn smiled, feeling relaxed and able to ignore minor irritations.

With a felt pen he changed the line connecting the two names into an arrow and added some other doodling, including a bull's-eye round Despain and an elaborate frame round the £3500. Gerald Despain's name lingered in his mind and seemed to have some special significance for him though he could not say what it was, and he could picture Despain quite clearly, recollected from a rogue's gallery of traitors who had assisted the Nazi cause. The French author Louis Ferdinand Céline was one of the group but he could not picture

Céline at all. The American poet Ezra Pound was another and he had a vague memory of Pound photographed with two GIs who had taken him prisoner. But why was it he could visualise Gerald Despain so well? Despain was tall and unusually handsome, with a shock of blonde hair and flashing teeth bared in a contemptuous expression, looking as if he didn't care if the world went hang—no doubt he had taken to the Nazi party like a duck to water.

Quinn stopped brooding on Despain and wondered how Moishe Eckstein had come to hear of the collection owned by a Mr Principle. He was not altogether surprised because Moishe was an unusual collector, more like a dealer in his get-up-and-go attitude in making additions to his collection. It was exactly a year since Moishe had strolled into the Books International premises and asked for Quinn's assistance in building an important collection of books and papers relating to the Holocaust. The importance of it, Moishe had stressed, was to lie in the 'tangential specialisation of the collection' which was to consist solely of material relating to anti-Semites of all nations but particularly those who had gone to Germany to assist the Nazi cause. To make the collection a permanent one Moishe had sold his garment business to fund it, and set up the Anna Krugman Foundation in memory of his mother-in-law who had been gassed in Treblinka. Moishe was in his late sixties with sparse white crinkly hair but a youthful face, often smiling, always lively and enthusiastic; his payments were by Sterling drafts and prompt. The perfect kind of customer in fact, but a very rare breed.

'Dee-da!' The door opened to this triumphal note and June entered the room carrying a tray with a steaming mug of coffee and a small pile of letters. 'I looked up lapis lazuli and it's a semi-precious stone...'

'Yes, but you're the rare, finest sapphire type. Is the Eckstein express packet there?'

'It is. So are we happier now? And the postman apologised. Said they're short-handed today because some men are off sick.'

'I know that sickness. It's called the Monday morning syndrome.'

'You're a hard man.' June put down the tray on Quinn's desk and pencilled a note:

'Cyril P has bought two books and is giving a third serious thought. He's spent £100 already.'

'All right. Give him a cup of coffee. And just one biscuit.'

'Hard—but fair.' June went out humming the Warsaw Concerto, something she was apt to do when things were going well.

The envelope from Eckstein was of catalogue size, covered with a plethora of airmail and express labels and written instructions 'Please rush.' The enclosed catalogue had shiny white card wrappers decorated on the front wrapper with a simple but eloquent sixteenth century engraving of one man handing money over to another who was counting on his fingers; squint-eyed and misshapen characters given charm by the engraver's art. Moishe's note was scrawled in green ink on an Anna S Krugman Foundation letter-heading:

Dear Jack,
    You missed out on this sale but that was probably due to it being held way out in Bucks county! The Despain collection was a steal at £2000! Do you think the ring was operating? Do you know Mr Principle? Is he a dealer?

Will he take a quick profit? Try him at £3000. Plus plus plus your usual percentage expenses whatever.

Cordially yours,
Moishe

The catalogue had been issued by Percy Younger & Son of Marlow, Bucks, a firm of whom Quinn had never heard. Looking quickly through it he saw that it was mostly of furniture and antiques with only a sprinkling of books and drawings; it was the kind of thing he might have overlooked. The Despain item was marked with a large green star and tick.

THE GERALD DESPAIN PAPERS

A LARGE COLLECTION OF ORIGINAL LETTERS, A DIARY, PAPERS, PHOTOGRAPHS, periodicals, etc, relating to the notorious traitor Gerald Despain who did propaganda work for the Nazis during the last war and who committed suicide in April, 1945.
During the 18th & 19th centuries the firm Despain & Co, Mediterranean merchants and money-lenders, was internationally known but virtually came to an

end with the death of Benjamin Despain, a shadowy figure about whom little is known. In 1895 Benjamin Despain married the Hon Evelyn Walters, a Victorian society beauty, and Gerald, their only child, was born in 1901. Benjamin Despain died in 1911. Gerald Despain was educated at Eton, Magdalen College and Sandhurst; he was commissioned in the Punjab Rifles in 1922 but cashiered the following year. During the 1920s he worked as a journalist in London and wrote two anti-Semitic pamphlets. In 1930 he went to Kenya and bought a farm but lived the life of a dissolute remittance man. This was in the 'Happy Valley' area of the White Highlands where some of his Eton contemporaries were then living. A joke of the period was 'Are you married or do you live in Kenya?' The Wanjohi river was said to run with cocktails and 'Cocaine was taken like snuff in Happy Valley.' In 1934 Gerald Despain joined the British Union of Fascists at the same time as his friend Lord Erroll. He was an habitué of the Muthaiga Country Club (where Jews were not allowed). At the outbreak of war in September 1939 he went to Berlin via Portugal. Throughout the war he did propaganda work for the Nazis, including writing pamphlets for distribution by the Luftwaffe. He was on friendly terms with highly placed members of the Nazi party and esteemed for his extreme anti-Semitic views. In 1943 he married Fraulein Herta Schellenberg and a son was born to them in 1944. In April 1945, knowing that the end of the war was imminent, Gerald Despain shot his wife and himself in their Hamburg apartment.

The letters can conveniently be considered in three groups.

(1) Early letters contained in a large wooden box. These include letters from his family when he was at Eton and Oxford. Also numerous letters to do with his career as a journalist and pamphleteer from a number of editors and minor authors of the period.

(2) Letters of the 'Happy Valley' period, in three card files. These include letters from the Prince of Wales, the Earl of Erroll, Lord Delamere, Karen Blixen,

Lord Francis Scott, Comte Frédéric de Janzé, Raymond de Trafford, Frank Greswold Williams (a notorious drug-dealer), Michael Lafone. There is also a group of letters from Alice de Janzé of whom her husband wrote in *Vertical Land:* 'No man will touch her exclusive soul, shadowy with memories, unstable, suicidal'.

(3) Letters of 1940–1945, preserved in a black metal deed-box, when Despain was living in Germany and various occupied European countries. Including letters from Adolph Hitler (two brief typed notes), Joseph and Magda Goebbels, Reichsmarschall Herman Göring, Heinrich Himmler, Rudolph Hess, Martin Bormann, Gerda Daranowsky Christian (Hitler's secretary, known as 'Dara'), Professor Karl Haushofer (the geo-politician), Gertraud Humps (Hitler's secretary, replacing 'Dara'), Gertraud Junge (known as 'Traudl') etc etc. Also a postcard from Edward, Duke of Windsor, signed 'Edward, Herzog von Windsor' (it was of the Duke of Windsor that Hitler said 'He's our greatest hope').

Another wooden box contains photographs and articles written by Despain in Britain in the 1920s; also articles in German in *Der Sturmer, Der Volkische Kurier, Deutsche Republik,* etc etc.

At the end of the description somebody had pencilled in the price obtained and the buyer's name called out at the sale as 'Principle, £2000'.

Quinn flicked through the catalogue, looking at the pencilled names of other buyers. Most of them were dealers he knew only slightly but the buyer of a set of Dickens in a fine binding was given as Harland, a good friend of his who had a shop in Cecil Court. Mickey Harland could be questioned about the identity of 'Principle' over the phone but Quinn was glad to have an excuse to leave his office and bustle about London which was the part of book-dealing he most enjoyed. He opened the rest of his letters and found they could be dealt with by June Whitall. In a matter of minutes he had dumped them on June's desk, said goodbye to her and Parkinson and left the premises of Books International. He was off on a quest, something that always quickened his step.

CHAPTER 8

'Oh sod it!' Mickey Harland said this automatically when he heard the door-bell of his shop and then laughed at himself. He thought: There's no pleasing me. I grumble when there is no business and I grumble when there is. In his early sixties he was becoming listless and apathetic like an old, run-down clock. 'Oh sod it!' and 'So what!' were becoming his daily litany.

Harland got up from his deck-chair by pressing hard on the arm-rests, a movement that would not have been necessary for him in former years, and walked quickly to the stairs which led from the crowded basement to the shop, intrigued by the fact that since hearing the bell there had been no other sound. He wondered what he would do if he discovered a shoplifter quietly at work. He thought it strange to find no-one in the shop until he realised that someone must have opened the door, changed their mind and instantly departed. It was just one more

70

irritating act by the great British public. Harland's assistant Miss Cathcart had only been away for a few days with 'flu but he silently prayed for her speedy return. She was always optimistic and positive, and had just the right approach for dealing with the public, something he definitely lacked.

Harland walked to the front door of the shop and looked down at the window display. As 1987 was the tri-centenary of the publication of Sir Isaac Newton's *Principia*, a fact which the Post Office had celebrated with a set of stamps, he thought it would be a good idea to have a window full of books by and about Newton. Miss Cathcart had set them out well, with informative price cards in her bold italic hand, but now the display was becoming dusty and two elastic bands holding volumes open and perished and looked like dead worms. Only one book had been sold and the display seemed to have attracted little attention. Harland opened his shop door and walked back in an effort to gauge the impression it made on the passer-by.

Most of the Newton volumes were bound in calf and that made the window a little dark, but Miss Cathcart had spaced the books out well, using the 1687 edition of *Principia* as a centre piece below which there was a large card with a quotation in her writing:

'The greatest achievement of seventeenth-century science was Newton's demonstration that the same force that makes the apple fall retains the planets in their courses.'

For a few moments Harland stood in his shop doorway and watched three people pass by without even glancing at his window and said quietly, 'To hell with them!' Entering the shop he saw that it was only 11 am—the morning was dragging and the physical work of clearing out the window, dusting and polishing was something that might speed the passing of time. After a cup of coffee, he thought, retreating downstairs. But no sooner had he put some water in the kettle than he heard the shop bell again. This time, however, he heard heavy steps and a voice he recognised calling out 'Miss Cathcart?' and then 'Mickey—are you skulking down there?' Harland put down the kettle and approached the stairs. Jack Quinn's large frame was at the top of them, craning down awkwardly. Quinn said, 'Can you spare me a few minutes Mickey? Just a couple of queries about that sale in Marlow—the one where you bought a set of Dickens.'

'Come on down, Jack. Miss Cathcart's away but I'm not exactly overwhelmed by business...'

'I like your Newton display. Very eye-catching.'

'That makes just you and me then. The British book-buying public are not being caught.'

'You did actually go to that sale in Marlow? Or did you send in a bid by post?'

'Oh yes, I went there, spent the best part of two days in those old-fashioned premises. Did the view on Thursday, then spent most of Friday morning at the sale, only buying one lot for my pains. Funny, I thought of you there because when I saw the Gerald Despain lot I remembered you saying that you had a keen customer for traitor material. Thought I might make myself a few quid by buying it and selling to you. There's a couple of stories about that sale if you're interested.'

'Tell me. I'm very interested.'

'Well, the first one is about the dodgy provenance of many of the items. Most of the interesting stuff there came from the house of the late Adrian Mackmurdo. During the war it seems that Mackmurdo was a major in the Intelligence Corps—I don't know what he did for the war effort but he certainly brought some loot back from Germany in '45. That Dickens set I bought for instance—there's a German bookplate in each volume, that of a Max Sauckel. What I want to know is, did Major Mackmurdo actually buy that set from Sauckel or did he just lift it from a bombed-out house? I'm not too happy about that, but then nobody was happy about the provenance of those things including your pal Dulau.'

'So Daniel was there...'

'Yes, a quite typical Daniel Dulau appearance. Bought just the one lot, a large folder of old engravings, right at the end of the sale. But, of course, it turned out to be the one great bargain. No wonder Dulau had a cat-who-ate-the-canary smile afterwards.'

'Why was that?'

'Well, it turns out there was a Rembrandt engraving, unique in that particular proof version, but only Dulau spotted it.'

'You said you had two stories about the sale.'

'Yes, but the other one is also about those engravings in a way. Seems that the catalogue was written up by Percy Younger's son Ralph or 'Mr Rafe' as the staff like to call him. Anyway, Ralph Younger did a description of the Gerald Despain material based on notes by the late Adrian Mackmurdo, and he took a very strong dislike to fascist Despain. The joke is you see that the Despain collection included just one photograph of Despain's papa, old Benjamin. Quite a striking looking chap, but bearded, hook-nosed and definitely a touch of the chosen race. You read that the Despain company were money-lenders? So that's why Ralph Younger chose the engraving of the Jewish money-lender for the cover of the catalogue. Rather neat I thought.'

'Did you see Mr Principle who bought the Despain papers?'

'I did indeed, sat quite close, but it was three people actually. At least there were three people who were in a huddle about the Despain lot, though a woman did all the bidding. In her late sixties, early

75

seventies—she didn't look at all well. Aided by a giant of a chap, about four inches taller than you, with extra wide shoulders and a mane of white hair, very straight back. I thought he must be ex-Army, probably a retired colonel, something like that. And a young man who seemed rather more detached about what was going on. But the woman was very excited and obviously unused to bidding, not quite sure what she was doing—she nearly bid against herself at one point.'

'So did you do any bidding?'

'Right at the start, took it up to one thousand pounds, but your pal Dulau put me off, shrugged his shoulders and whispered that I was wasting my time as "Mr Principle" had tons of money. "Serious money", as he put it. So I gave up.'

'Then Daniel must know the bidder?'

'It seemed like that but it's always hard to be sure about anything where Master Dulau's involved.'

'I know just what you mean, but it's probably worthwhile having a word with him.'

'I wish you luck old man, but bear in mind what I said about the provenance.

Even if the trio are willing to re-sell the lot, do they legally own it? You saw that Gerald Despain had a son in 1944? Then surely the son is the real owner? Major Mackmurdo probably carted off the stuff from the Despain flat during some Intelligence Corps foray at the end of the war...'

'It's a good point, but for all we know Despain's son may be dead too. Anyway I'll cross that bridge if I have any success in finding the trio.'

CHAPTER 9

When Quinn returned to his office he found that June Whitall had gone out for an early lunch, leaving a 'Back at 12.45' notice propped up on the door handle. There was a pile of books on the long table to be catalogued, and various routine matters of business requiring attention, but a vague restlessness made it impossible for him to settle to these tasks. He found that he could think of nothing but the quest for the Despain papers and the identity of the trio who had come together at Marlow to buy them.

After only a few minutes Quinn left the Books International premises and set off for Albemarle Street, where Daniel Dulau had his art gallery and offices in a handsome building which he was rumoured to own. There were all kinds of rumours about Daniel Dulau in the world of dealers, largely inspired by envy and jealousy because of the quite remarkable success he had achieved in a few years. He was said to be queer and to have a tough south London boyfriend, but it was also said that he had a rather plain wife whom he kept hidden in the West Country and a beautiful mistress living in Bayswater. Another story was that Dulau kept a file on all the people with whom he did business, listing their peccadilloes. Quinn's relationship with Dulau was not, he believed, affected by jealousy, but it was certainly ambivalent owing to Dulau's complicated nature. Dulau was tall and slim with black hair, and he had nearly perfect teeth which he displayed a lot in smiles as if everything went well for him. Madeleine considered that Dulau was 'charming', an adjective she rarely

78

used. Certainly Dulau had exceptional energy, being willing to work seven days a week with an extra long day on Sunday, something that Quinn could not do. He was also extremely shrewd and perceptive. He was the only person, apart from Madeleine, who had criticised Quinn to his face, but he did this in a disarming way by always coupling himself with the criticism: 'You're like me Jack, you think you can buy your way out of trouble.' 'You're like me Jack, you think there's nothing to life except work, food, drink and a bit of the other.' 'You're like me Jack, you're loath to change yourself.' In fact Dulau had displayed a remarkable ability to change himself, much complaining of shyness and migraine headaches when he first started dealing but later enjoying robust health in running a thriving West End gallery. There was a period, some years before, when Quinn had been able to do quite a lot of business with him, at a time when Dulau particularly favoured deals for cash, saying 'Let's not complicate matters with book-keeping', but then he had soared off into another sphere where it was rumoured he was supported by a merchant bank. Suddenly he acquired wealthy show-biz customers and was said to have 'a tame millionaire in tow'. Charlie Saunders, Quinn's oldest dealer friend, summed up Dulau by saying, 'He's so sharp, he'll cut hisself.'

Walking up Hay Hill Quinn's steps slowed, not because of the slight incline but because he had second thoughts as he so often did about approaching Dulau. After a visit to the gallery he usually found himself wrong-footed, having said too much and learnt precious little. He walked along Dover Street undecided whether to call in at the gallery or not and then was trapped by its striking window display of two paintings by James Tissot, one a view of the Thames from Shadwell and the other of two fashionable women, their heads close together, sharing a confidence. There was a hand-lettered explanatory card between the paintings: 'After making an auspicious start in Paris as a painter of elegant society women James Tissot became involved in the Commune and had to take refuge in London in 1871. Both of our paintings date from the period 1871-3.'

He tentatively opened the gallery door and was greeted by a new female face who said, 'Good morning, Mr Quinn, can

I help you?' Once more he was puzzled by Dulau's rapid turnover in assistants all of whom seemed to be in the same mould, tallish, blondish and very sophisticated. He was also puzzled that the girl should know him but then realised that she was probably ex-Sotheby's. 'I was hoping to see Daniel. Is he about?' He expected excuses or delays but, again to his surprise, the blonde girl said, 'Will you go on up. I think he's expecting you. You know it's the third floor?'

'Right, thanks. I say, what a nice window, the Tissots!' The girl smiled but did not deign to reply to his comment, obviously thinking it a cliché. Quinn entered the old-fashioned lift which ascended ponderously to the dismal sound of rattling chains. Before he opened the lift door at the third floor he heard a tinkling piano and when he entered Dulau's private sanctum it was to find a new acquisition in place, a piano-player which Dulau was playing, with flourishes, and crooning 'Bye-bye blackbird.'

'Morning, Daniel. Thriving as usual?'

'Jack! How nice!' Dulau said this, spinning round on his piano stool and looking as if he had been scrubbed and polished from head to toe. His shirt, cardigan, tie and trousers were in various shades of grey; his black shoes gleamed, as did his hair. He grinned and said 'Are we going to do some biz, Jack?'

'Alas, no. I'm going to waste your time, I'm afraid...'

'Waste away.' Dulau's quick glance took in the Marlow auction catalogue which Quinn was carrying. 'Ah yes, the Percy Younger sale. I remember that Mickey Harland said you might be interested in the Despain papers. You're like me Jack, when you latch on to something you really go for it.'

'That's right. I want to track down the people who bought the collection. Do you think I'm wasting my time?'

'Hard to say Jack. I vaguely knew the face of the woman concerned, knew she had money at least. Probably just a face I'd seen thumbing through the *Tatler*. But I can put a name to the big chap with her; he's General Erskine—he's in *Who's Who*. However I'm sure it was the woman bought the lot, her friends were only there to advise her. You see, when the hammer fell Erskine said, "There you are, my dear, it's all yours."'

'Well thanks. I can fall back on the General perhaps, if I can't track down the woman. But first I think I'll try the auction firm.'

'Yes, that's an idea, but don't bother with Percy Younger Esquire, he's as straight as his back. You'll do better with the sales clerk, a fat man called Ted Smiles. I should think he can be bought, and probably just for a big box of chocs.'

'Sorry about taking up your time, Daniel. I know you're a busy chap.'

Dulau put his right hand behind him so that it rested on the keys of the piano-player. 'Ah, now you're being ironic Jack! But seriously, I like talking about that sale. Not at all a run-of-the-mill affair, quite fascinating in fact. Of course if the auctioneers had known their business and advertised the sale properly the place would have been packed. It had all kinds of appeal, that odd bunch who lived in Happy Valley, their raffish lives of dope and drink, and that despicable Despain character...'

Dulau left the sentence hanging unfinished, his dark intelligent face set for once in an unhappy, thoughtful expression; like that he rather resembled a portrait of Spinoza, and it struck Quinn that Dulau

83

might have Jewish blood himself. Quinn said, 'Mickey thought you were rather concerned about the provenance of the Mackmurdo stuff, that it might all be "liberated" loot.'

Dulau laughed. 'Not really, I was being naughty. I raised that phantom just before the sale to give everyone something to think about. But it's nothing—I mean, it might be difficult in 1987 to prove that Major Mackmurdo actually bought those odds and ends in 1945 but it would be just as hard to prove that he didn't have title to them.'

'And you think that's the case with the Despain papers?'

'Ah, there you find the chink in my armour! No, I can't imagine that money changed hands over that acquisition. Anyway, I'm very happy with my purchase. Not so much with the Rembrandt proof, believe it or not, as with the engraving of the money-lender! It's of Durer-like quality but by an unknown artist. And one in the eye for the ghastly Gerald! Did Mickey tell you that the only photograph of Benjamin Despain looked as if he might be of Jewish stock? It seems that Gerald took after his honourable mama, a statuesque blonde beauty, guaranteed one hundred per cent Aryan.'

'I must be going. Off to Marlow, I think.'

'That's it. And let me know how you get on—whether you have any success with the sad-looking lady or General Erskine—I should think he'll be a tough nut to deal with. Now, don't forget, search out Ted Smiles at Marlow. He's your best bet.'

CHAPTER 10

Jack Quinn drove into Marlow feeling hungry, slightly edgy and sharp as a tack. Which was better, he mused, than feeling somnolent with food and drink. That was the positive side to having missed lunch. Before commencing his drive from London he had looked into a pub, fancying a pint and a sandwich, but the bar had been full of cigarette smoke and the noise of a score of conversations going on at once. It was over forty-eight hours since Quinn had drunk any alcohol and he acknowledged that it did make a difference to how he felt; Dr McGovern had been right in stressing that alcohol did not mix well with the tablets he took for sinus trouble—the same advice was printed on the packet but he had always ignored it, thinking his constitution tough enough to overcome such trifles.

When Quinn got out of his old Mercedes, which he parked in a road leading away from the bridge over the Thames, he felt as if all his senses were heightened. Raucous cries of seagulls wheeling above the bridge made him look up and study the mackerel coloured sky where grey clouds were being driven by a strong wind from west to east, swirling about as if in a frenzy. Then his eye was taken by a tiny woman with doll-like hands struggling into a child-size mac; he absorbed the impression of foreboding on the face of an old man whose hair was shorn to a black shadow on his skull; he noticed a girl with a scarf sea-green and purple like a peacock's neck.

The premises of 'Percy Younger & Son—Auctioneers—Established 1934' were sited in Marlow's busiest shopping street, and looked like an old chapel which had been skilfully converted. Glossy dark green and gold paint gave the impression of a prosperous concern and the date 1934 added the assurance of stability and tradition. Quinn opened the double front door to find a corridor of gleaming green rubber flooring, with offices on either side leading down to the glass doors of the saleroom where porters were at work moving furniture about. Fluorescent lighting made everything appear to be tinged a sickly green. A middle-aged woman with faded blonde hair gave him a wary, professional smile. 'Yes?'

'I was hoping to see Mr Smiles.'

The faded blonde peered at her wristwatch and said, 'Oh yes, Ted should be back by now. Third door. If not, then just knock on Mr Rafe's door—he's bound to know where Ted is.'

Quinn walked past an open door and heard a tall man say: 'Trouble is he's a 30-watt bulb in a 100-watt socket.'

The third door was lettered in gilt: 'E Morgan Smiles—Sales Manager'. When Quinn knocked there was a long pause before a thick voice said irritably, 'Yes? What is it?'

The door opened to disclose an unusually fat man wearing a clerical grey suit, seated behind a cluttered desk on which stood a bottle of Coca-cola and a half-eaten Mars bar. He looked as if he was sweating with a greasy forehead, and his small brown eyes darted back and forth as if he were seeking a route of escape.

'Mr Smiles? My name's Jack Quinn. I'm a rare book dealer and I wanted to have a word about the Major Mackmurdo sale.'

The fat man sniffed in air deeply and visibly swelled with self-importance. He folded his hands over a gross stomach. 'Yes, I see. Funny thing about that sale. *Now* people are interested and we get all the publicity. Talk about the cart before the horse! Of course I tried to tell the old man we were on to a winner there but would he listen? Now we're even getting enquiries from Fleet Street and I wouldn't be surprised if the TV cameras turned up here. And what good will that do? Like asking the king's men to put Humpty-Dumpty together again.'

'I'm very interested in the Gerald Despain papers.'

'Aren't they all! Well, it was lot forty-six in the sale, sold to a Mr Principle for two oh oh oh netto. No buyer's premium.'

'But who is Mr Principle?'

Smiles stooped awkwardly to pick up

a bulky folio ledger from the floor. His voice deepened dramatically: 'You mean the name duly entered in here? The actual name and address of the buyer who preferred to remain pseudonymous? Oh no can do colonel!' Smiles stood up as if to accentuate the impossibility of this request and inferring that the palaver was over; his presence in the small room was overwhelming. He pressed down hard on the ledger as if trying to glue it to his desk. 'One has one's principles and one sticks to them, if you'll excuse the pun.' It was a routine reply, polished by repetition.

Quinn reached into the inner pocket of his jacket where he kept some ten pound notes, saying, 'Yet I suppose money talks.' He took out three of the notes and formed them into a triangle on the desk.

'I suppose it does.' Smiles hovered heavily over the desk. His suit was two sizes too small for him and his feet bulged out of black patent leather shoes. He raised a meaty hand to shield his mouth and spoke in a stage whisper, 'Could you make a square of those?'

'Afraid not. Just the triangle.'

'I see.' After a few moments hesitation Smiles made the notes disappear into his jacket, whispering, 'See page one oh five.' In a loud voice he said, 'So, I'll just pop along to the saleroom and check if that piece is there.'

At the door he whirled round, surprisingly light on his feet. 'Be discreet, eh, skipper?'

The ledger listed items sold at the sales in a tiny but perfectly legible hand. Usually just a name was given when items were bought by dealers, but there were a few addresses. On page 105 lot 46 was bracketed with a name and address: Mrs Rex Vavasour, Highmoor Hall, Rotherfield Greys, Oxon.

CHAPTER 11

The phone was ringing in Quinn's mews-house when he parked his Mercedes in the garage below it. 'Keep on ringing, shan't be a sec,' he said, slamming on the brake. Phone calls at his new private address were few and far between. Without any good reason he hoped the call might be from Madeleine asking him round to the Barton Street house to talk things over.

In his haste Quinn fumbled with the front door key and stumbled on the first tread of the staircase as he tried to race up to the phone. It stopped ringing just before he picked it up. Nevertheless he held it close to his ear and muttered 'Damn,' thinking about the prospect of another lonely and uninteresting evening before him. He was annoyed with himself for missing the call and pointlessly angry with everything. He contrasted his mood with the one of non-specific gratitude he had felt when having supper at Remenham and taking his daughters home on the Sunday evening. He wanted to have them about him again, chattering and laughing. As he replaced the mute phone he said bitterly, 'I never appreciated anything when I had it' wishing that the rare confession might work some magic in putting things back to where they had been before his final row with Madeleine.

He sagged mentally and physically as he went into the kitchen and selected a bottle of red Rioja from the rickety old wine-rack he had inherited from a previous tenant. Above the wine-rack he had propped up a quotation from the poet John Gay and he read it aloud:

'Fill every glass, for wine inspires us
And fires us
With courage and joy.
Women and wine should life employ.
Is there ought else on earth desirous?'

He took the card from its precarious position and crumpled it up, with a heavy sigh. Wine and women had brought him to his present position—Madeleine had ignored his drinking and philandering for years, and then had decided that enough was enough. And now that the philanderer was set free, with what amounted to a bachelor existence, he found it was not what he really wanted. And the only attempt at love-making in the Bourdon Street bedroom had proved a fiasco—so much so that he had been reminded of a headline he once read in the *Daily Mail:* Rubirosa was fizzle in bed, Latin beauty said.'

Quinn opened the Rioja and poured a large tumbler of the wine he always found to his taste. After an alcohol-free weekend it seemed particularly good. He sat at the kitchen table and doodled on the back of the letter his daughters had left for him.

He drew a spider's web with a little box at the centre which he inscribed 'The Gerald Despain papers', then added three blobs on the web which he thought of as representing Mrs Rex Vavasour, General Erskine and their male companion at the sale in Marlow. He changed one of the blobs into the head of a man with a military peaked cap. 'You can draw quite well, daddy!' Dolly had once said in a tone of surprise, and it was true that he could do useful little sketches in planning the covers for the catalogues issued three times a year by Books International. 'To phone Mrs Vavasour now or not to phone?' he asked aloud. The question sounded over-loud and funny in the empty flat—if he continued to live alone talking to himself would become a habit. He altered another of the blobs so that it vaguely resembled a woman's head. 'No, leave it until the morning.' He realised that the call to Mrs Vavasour would have to be carefully phrased and diplomatic and a little vague so that he did not sound too much like a dealer trying to get his foot in the front door. And he did not feel in a careful, diplomatic mood. Unlike Dulau, he thought. Daniel always seemed to be diplomatic, 'charming', as Madeleine said, equable and imperturbable—all the qualities he lacked and reasons why he would never obtain great success like Daniel D. Suddenly he remembered Dulau saying that General Erskine was to be found listed in *Who's Who*. The current issue was in his Davies Street office but he had kept the 1984 edition with a few other old reference books at the Barton Street house, so Madeleine would have placed it—no doubt with pleasure—in one of the cartons she had packed for him.

As he walked through the door of the living-room he spied the heavy scarlet-bound volume at the top of a carton. Erskine's entry was impressively long, taking up nearly half a column.

ERSKINE, General James Hugh, KCB 1970 (CB 1966): CBE 1962; DSO 1945; MC 1940; b 10 Aug 1910; er s of late Colonel William James Erskine DSO, Lowes House, by Clunie, Perthshire; m 1938 Louise er d of late Air Commodore Sir Thomas Etchells. Educ Eton, Christ Church, Oxford. 2nd Lieut Scots Guards, 1932. Served War of 1939-45 in France, Italy and NW Europe...

Quinn's eyes flitted down five lines of ranks and positions held by the distinguished General up to 1970 and fastened on the entry at the end, Erskine's address in 1984: Nantyffin Lodge, Nr Crickhowell, Powys, Wales. As he noted it down he found he was whistling the song 'Too late now', stopped and mentally kicked himself all the way from Bourdon Street to Barton Street. The phone rang again to stop this and he walked through to it, mentally rehearsing what to say if it was Madeleine.

When he picked it up he heard faint background music and a female voice asked nervously, 'Is that you, Jacky?' The name Jacky told him that it was Lilian Saunders calling; she had known him since he was a child and was the only person to call him 'Jacky' as Charlie Saunders was the only man who ever called him 'Jacko'.

'Lilian? Yes, it's me, anything wrong?'

'Sorry to bother you dear, but I'm worried about Charlie. He hasn't been home since Friday evening. You know

95

what he's like, always driving off to some sale or other, or to do a deal, but he usually phones me—he's good about that.'

'Yes, I know, but I haven't seen him for about a week...'

'A week! But I thought he was seeing you on that Friday evening—he's got it written down in his diary. Listen—he put "Sept 25th, Sotheby's party—ask Jacko about the Pickering Place party and meeting the terrible duo". I was sure you must have seen him on Friday...'

'Well, Lil, I'm ashamed to tell you but on Friday evening I got very drunk somewhere, passed out and ended up in hospital.'

'Oh Jacky! Did you hurt yourself dear?'

'No-nothing except my pride. But it was a lesson I can tell you, coming round in a hospital ward afterwards. I'm going to try to learn from it. So I suppose it's possible I did see Charlie that evening. Perhaps I had too much to drink at the Sotheby's party—the trays of wine come round rather frequently there. But I can't remember anything about Pickering Place—I don't think I've even heard of it.'

'Well, what do you think I should do?'

Quinn could visualise Lilian standing

and fretting in her kitchen where there was a wall-phone. The Saunders owned a large, comfortable house in The Vale at Golders Green. The house was too large really for a childless couple but Charlie was apt to use it as a kind of extra store-room for furniture and objets d'art which he was willing to sell if sufficiently tempted. Lou Samuel, the silver dealer, said that everything in Charlie's house except Lilian was for sale 'at a price'. Lilian seemed to spend much of her life alone in the kitchen, kept company by her Persian cat Sam and a wireless.

'Has Charlie got any business appointments for this week in his diary?'

'A sale at Phillips on Thursday.'

'Oh, ten to one he'll be back for that. Now try not to worry. He's probably fine. If he'd had an accident in the BMW you would have heard from the Police. I'll phone this time tomorrow evening and if he's not back by then I'll call round for a chat.'

'Thanks dear. Till tomorrow then.'

As Quinn replaced the phone a glaring light seemed to flare in the wasteland of his mind and he visualised Charlie talking to him somewhere, arguing persuasively about going to a party: 'It'll be something unusual. Besides there's a bloke I want you to meet. There's a special reason,' he had said, ending up with a knowing wink as he was apt to do when predicting something good.

Quinn poured himself another glass of wine and sat down by the kitchen table, straining to remember other events of the shrouded Friday evening. No more images of Charlie Saunders came into his mind but he found it easier to picture the tall blonde girl who had stood by his side and talked in a mocking voice and had a silvery laugh. A Botticelli-like beauty with unusually large sea-green eyes and an enigmatic smile, as if she knew some amusing secret. He remembered putting his arm round her tiny waist—it had not been repulsed but he had sensed it was not welcome and had withdrawn it. That was when she began to refer to him as 'Jeremy Fisher'. He struggled to remember something about the Beatrix Potter story. What had the frog Jeremy Fisher done? Nothing much that he could recall apart from going fishing for minnows and being caught by a big trout and taken to the bottom of a pond. Quinn knew that he could never be considered good-looking but he was equally sure that he did not resemble a frog. What else was there about the blonde girl? She was tall, slim and elegant. He pictured her hand wearing an unusual ring. She wore a peacock-blue dress that went with her eyes. And someone had called her 'Tommy'. That was very odd but he was sure that it had happened, and that the girl had hurried away from his side without another word to him. Then an image of Charlie came into his mind, Charlie gulping a digitalis tablet and swallowing some liquid. Quinn thought hard but his capricious memory would not release any more secrets.

CHAPTER 12

Tom lay well back in a dark brown leather armchair with his long legs outstretched. The chair was a comfortable one and Tom looked very much at home though in fact he was seated in the entrance hall to a large flat in Stanhope Terrace to which he had made a forced entry. The flat belonged to Francesco Manservigi who owned the Naples gambling club. It was 2.30 am and Tom had forced the front door to the flat because he wanted to be waiting when the professional gambler returned from his club—to give him a nasty surprise. Manservigi had come to London from Naples as a fully fledged member of the notorious *Nuova Camorra Organizzata,* with an ugly reputation; reputed to have had more than one enemy shut up all night in the drying room of a laundry, and others buried in concrete. Now Manservigi had made an enemy of Tom who was a more fitting opponent.

Manservigi's flat was at once luxurious and faintly gloomy, furnished with dark oak-panelled walls and brown fitted carpets dimly lit by indirect overhead lighting. There were old steel engravings on the walls of the hall which Tom took to be of Naples and its surrounding area. On a Bluthner piano in the large living-room there was just one photograph, in a gold frame, of an ugly old woman with a lipless face much like Manservigi's; otherwise it was an impersonal place, a suitable home for a man whose sole interest was money. By Tom's armchair there was a small table bearing a cream-coloured telephone, and a table-lamp which threw a pool of light around Tom's legs stretched out on either side of his black leather briefcase. The case stood open to disclose rubber gloves, a lead cosh swathed in black velvet, and a short length of electric flex one end of which was attached to a plug. The other end of the flex had been bared to expose inch-long ends of bare wire. As Tom looked down into the case the things inside gave him a quiet feeling of satisfaction, showing a job well planned. Tom wore a grey flannel suit and from an inner pocket he extracted a small piece of paper bearing notes relating to death, a subject which obsessed Tom and was always at the back of his mind no matter how pleasing or interesting his momentary diversions might be. He glanced through the notes: '...the more vascular areas of the skin offer the least resistance. Metallization may take place. "Ventricular fibrillation"—an uncontrollable twitching of the muscular wall of the heart which stops the heart's rhythmic beat and is generally fatal. If no attempt is made to revive the victim the state of the suspended animation will pass imperceptibly into death.'

'Mr Tod' glanced at his wrist-watch and extended his left hand, on which he wore a silver death's-head signet ring, towards the front door that he had carefully closed after forcing the lock, and urged 'Tommy Brock' to return, 'Come on, come on, come on!'

'Coming to a permanent arrangement' with someone was always a tricky business, the dangers of which Tom never underestimated. He always did his homework well on such occasions and took all reasonable precautions to cover himself. In the case of Manservigi he had spent some hours, both late at night and early in the morning, timing the gambling club owner's return to his flat. If 'Tommy Brock' was to break the pattern and unexpectedly return with a girl or a bit of rough trade then 'Mr Tod's' plan would have to be aborted, and apologies made about the forced lock, an eventuality which Tom regarded like having to swallow a toad, but he would do it if he must because he only survived in a dangerous world, following a dangerous trade, by always being practical. 'Mr Tod' said quietly, 'But if I read your mind right, "Tommy Brock", sex means nothing to you and you'll be alone, as usual!'

Moments after this prediction Tom's reverie was rudely broken by the front door flying open and Manservigi, half falling, half running into the room, appearing as if he might explode with anger.

'What the fuck you doin'? How the hell you get in here?'

Manservigi was a heavily built man with short legs and long arms, dapper in a dinner jacket and wearing a black trilby. He closed the door behind him with one hand and swept off the trilby with the other to disclose a widow's peak of glossy black hair. He seemed out of breath. Rage made his eyes appear black. Tom was not at all disconcerted—he remained seated with an unreadable expression, his hands together in his lap, twiddling his thumbs. He smiled faintly as he replied, 'I do have this talent for opening doors.'

'That's something that could prove to be a fatal mistake one day.'

Tom leant forward to fish about in his briefcase and produced what appeared to be a thick wad of fifty pound notes, held in a tight roll by a black elastic band. 'I owe you some cash.'

Manservigi appeared puzzled and ran a hand across his swarthy face. 'I know you do, but I don't want you breakin' in here in the middle of the night to pay me. I'm a very private person. This place here,' he gestured in the direction of the living-room as if invoking the memory of his mother, 'is sacred.'

Tom raised his eyebrows. 'I see. Well, that's just how I feel about Tommy. *Nothing* can be allowed to worry her. Yet you sent round two of your heavies to call on us and they threatened her—tried to frighten her.'

Manservigi said something *sotto voce* in Italian and waved his hand to dismiss the possibility of threats. 'You mean Miss Tamsin? No, nothing personal with her. Just business. The cash was overdue.'

Tom held the roll of notes high in the air. 'You see I always pay my debts, *coûte-que-coûte.*' He tossed the wad towards Manservigi. The throw was perfectly judged, like everything he did, with just enough power not to reach Manservigi's outstretched hand. Tom pointed the hand wearing the signet ring at the gambler, as if blessing or cursing him. 'Go on, count it! I shall want a receipt.'

Manservigi took a step forward and bent down to pick up the notes. As he did

Tom leapt forward snatching up the lead cosh and hit the gambler on the side of the head. Manservigi prostrated himself on his arms as if he was a Muslim at prayer. Within a minute Tom was wearing his rubber gloves and heaving Manservigi into the armchair by the small table. As soon as the gambler was seated Tom unplugged the table-lamp and inserted the plug at the end of the short flex. Manservigi showed no sign of regaining consciousness, slumped in the chair, eyes closed, a dribble of liquid coming from his thin mouth. Tom put the bare ends of the flex in Manservigi's mouth and then used a sticky plaster to keep it closed. He rearranged the gambler's limp body at ease in the armchair, smiled at the sight,and used his foot to switch on the electric current in the flex. For a moment he had the impression of an aura of blue fire about Manservigi's head: though the gambler's body remained inert his big hands tried to protest about such treatment and made finger sketches in the air. Then the heavy body jerked convulsively and the dark eyes opened with an awful expression.

Tom took two steps back to regard his handiwork but he was not the kind of person to linger in such circumstances. Once a job was done he believed in quitting the scene as soon as possible. He noted Manservigi's burnt lips and nightmare expression with satisfaction, but the artist in him told him that something was missing. He looked round the room and realised what it was. Moments later he threw the trilby hat so that it landed, only slightly askew, on Manservigi's sleek head. Tom pouched the roll of cut-up paper disguised by one fifty-pound note, put the cosh into his briefcase and left the flat, being careful to wear the rubber gloves while opening and closing the front door. As he left he murmured, 'Addio, Francesco!'

CHAPTER 13

Tuesday morning, September 29th, 1987

A day of deluging rain and dramatic clouds and busy windscreen wipers on the M4. The wipers on Quinn's old Mercedes behaved eccentrically, sometimes doing

their job efficiently but at other times
hesitating as if the work was all too much
for them. As soon as Quinn turned off
the M4 onto the A423 to Oxfordshire he
pulled into the side of the road to give
them a rest and have a break himself, and
munch a delicious looking pear which he
had brought as a kind of breakfast, and
think once more about what he should say
to Mrs Rex Vavasour. Moishe Eckstein
had envisaged a simple deal in which
'Mr Principle' might be willing to take a
quick profit of fifteen hundred pounds on
the Despain collection, but since Daniel
Dulau had identified Mrs Vavasour as
having 'serious money' that seemed to
be out of the question. If she proved to
be a rich fascist sympathiser who admired
Despain's anti-Semitism, then the chance
of buying any of the papers was remote; but
there were all kinds of possibilities which
could only be resolved by meeting her.

Quinn looked at the map and saw he
was only a few miles away from Highmoor
which was in the Chiltern Hills area. Mrs
Vavasour had agreed, in an attractive 'little
girl' voice, to see him 'any time after eleven
am. I'm hopeless before eleven.' His watch
showed it to be 11.15. After two miles of

winding road he stopped to ask the way from an old man with a forward-jutting thatch of silver hair who was working in a ditch.

'The Hall?' the old man repeated, giving Quinn a sharp look. 'You'll want Mrs Vav'sour then?'

'Yes, please.'

'I see.' The man looked searchingly at Quinn as if trying to estimate whether he might be a lawful visitor to Highmoor Hall. 'Well, see here,' he said slowly, 'this road, it forks left and right after about half a mile. Just then you'll see the lodge and the lodge gates on your left—a boarded-up small house. That's the start of the drive but you won't get far along it in that car. Some of the poplars are down and Mrs Vav'sour, she only just manages it by dodging about in her Mini. So you'll have to park by the lodge. Shame about them Lombardy poplars—that drive used to look a picture.'

'Many thanks.'

There were hints that Mrs Vavasour must be somewhat eccentric in being willing to spend money on the Despain papers but not to have the poplars removed from her drive; this was the kind of thing that added zest to Quinn's encounters in his dealing career.

The lodge looked quite derelict with faded chalk graffiti on some of the boarded-up windows, slates missing from the roof and one chimney precariously poised as if about to fall. Quinn parked his car and looked up the drive, and saw that the old man had not exaggerated the difficulties of driving along it. His eye was taken by a faded and torn Union Jack flapping in a desultory manner at the top of a white pole rising from a lawn of uncut grass. On the other side of the drive the poplars bordered a hard tennis court behind badly rusted wire netting. The tennis net had split at the centre and had been left where it lay, while couch-grass sprouted through the pitted red grit surface of the court. It looked like the ideal place for Gillian Strachey to play and claim all kinds of local rules.

At the end of the drive Quinn could see no sign of dereliction about the large house that confronted him, a handsome building of grey stone with tall gables and spiralling chimneys which he thought would be of the Edwardian epoch. The front door stood open but Quinn rat-tatted on it and pulled on an old bell. After a few moments a feminine voice called out, 'Come through Mr Quinn. Do come in.'

Quinn entered the hall. A broad staircase led up to a gallery and a ginger cat eyed him warily from the top stair. The house smelt faintly of damp and cats. A tray of cat-litter stood near the stairs and a large black cat limped away to the back of the hall. A mounted lion's head looked down on the stairs but the hall was dominated by the three-quarter length portrait in oils of a man wearing white flannels and an MCC yellow and red blazer; he had curly hair, a long nose and a rosebud mouth. Lettering on a gilt panel proclaimed the portrait to be of 'Rex Vavasour, MP, 1903-1980'. Near to the painting an oak-panelled door stood ajar and through it Quinn could hear Mrs Vavasour's girlish voice.

'Skills darling? I don't ask for skills! Just some idiot youth who will sit on the mower and pretend he's at Brooklands or Brands Hatch or whatever. Jumbo was here the other day, d'you see. Didn't say anything but his keen eye never misses a trick. And I could see he was shocked. Usually I think oh what the hell but I can't be upsetting the dear old boy...' The voice's tone changed and she said, 'In here Mr Quinn,' in a peremptory way.

Quinn walked through the doorway into a large drawing-room with french windows opening onto the wet, jungly garden and a splendid view of fields and woods under an ink-black cloud. Mrs Vavasour lay on a beige-coloured couch in front of a struggling log fire. She wore a black frock and a cream cardigan. She was small and pale with dark brown hair dragged back from her face which she had made up in a garish fashion with a Joan Crawford lipsticked mouth and green eyelids. Her dark brown eyes had discoloured whites, and she gave the impression of a long-time invalid who spent much of her life on the couch, letting the world go by. In her right hand she held a white telephone, in her left a tall glass of clear liquid which Quinn suspected was gin rather than water. She stared at him myopically as though trying to get him into focus, and raised the lipsticked glass in salutation.

Into the telephone she said patiently, 'Yes, darling, I do know that. Yes, darling, I see...' She pulled a funny face to show that she was growing tired of the conversation which Quinn sensed

111

might have turned into a lecture directed at her, and for a moment he had a glimpse of the gamin-like girl she once must have been. She used the back of her left hand to stifle a theatrical yawn. 'Yes, darling, I'll try...I know, I know...Oh, so Geoffrey says that...'

Quite deliberately she coughed straight into the mouthpiece, a phlegmy cough which sounded as if it might be difficult to control. She said, 'Oh, I'm sorry darling, I just have to say goodbye, rest my throat. Yes, goodbye my dear.'

Mrs Vavasour replaced the telephone on its stand at her feet and struggled up from the couch, extending her right hand vaguely in Quinn's direction. Her movements were slow, almost soporific. Quinn saw that there were three wine cartons at the far end of the couch and that the fire was struggling to consume pieces of paper and envelopes. Mrs Vavasour produced a smile with a lot of effort behind it. 'Well Mr Quinn?' the greeting had been selected to exclude any warmth. 'So you are a book-dealer.'

'That's right.'

'Something I know nothing about, the world of dealers. But Rex used to buy antique books, from a Mr Basil Blackwell in Oxford. You know Mr Blackwell?'

'I know the firm.'

'Rex used to talk about the man he dealt with there, but until I went to that sale I'd never met a dealer.'

'You did buy the Despain papers at the Mackmurdo sale?'

'That's right. But it was supposed to be quite private, a secret, you see, and now the whole world seems to know about it. Some young reporter with the gutter press phoned me up, tried to lecture me about Gerald. A traitor! For God's sake, poor old Gerry shot himself! Isn't that punishment enough? But how did you hear about me Mr Quinn? Was there something in the papers?'

Quinn decided to protect Ted Smiles. 'A friend of mine, another dealer, at the Mackmurdo sale—he recognised you.'

'Really!' Mrs Vavasour sounded unconvinced. 'Well, do come and sit down, Mr Quinn. Relax, I shan't eat you.' She sat down heavily right at the end of the couch and Quinn joined her. He could smell gin on her breath and a musky perfume. She looked thoughtfully at him and said, 'You know, whenever I hear the word book I prick up my ears—I mean, I'm always on the *qui vive* for someone who will write...' She gestured over her shoulder at a large photograph, in a silver frame, standing on a Steinway baby grand. 'Someone good enough to do Rex's biography. It's a fascinating story! Such an interesting life you know.'

Quinn made a point of studying the photograph of her late husband which showed him looking rather pleased with himself. Half a dozen other photographs of him, all in silver frames, were on display around the room—there was even one on a cluttered drinks trolley. Rex Vavasour seemed to like being photographed in profile. When Quinn turned back he noticed that a violet envelope, addressed in green ink to Gerald Despain Esq, was darkening on the fire and threatening to burst into flames. Mrs Vavasour noticed his look and smiled. 'My privilege Mr Quinn! I purchased the letters quite legally, all above board. So now they're mine and I'm free to do as I choose...' 'Dead, dead, dead!' she added with vehemence. 'A world of ghosts, all those dear people Gerry and Rex and I knew. Where are they now? Just a world of ghosts!' She made an ugly grimace which showed teeth too good to be true. 'But what's your interest in these old letters? Surely you're too young to have known any of the people involved?'

'No personal interest. A customer of mine in New York wanted me to enquire and see if there was a chance that any of the collection might be resold.'

'What a strange idea! Surely he must realise I'm a private individual, not a dealer. Is your American customer a Jewish gentleman, by any chance?'

The way the phrase 'Jewish gentleman' was accented slightly nettled Quinn but he let it pass and said, 'Yes, he is a Jew. The Nazis killed his mother-in-law in the camp at Treblinka.'

'Oh God!' Mrs Vavasour made an odd gesture with her right fist, like a blow aimed at her heart. 'Is poor old Gerry going to be pilloried in New York now—are all his private things to be put on show? I mean for God's sake—Gerry didn't pitchfork Jews into ovens—all he did was write some silly pamphlets.'

Quinn shrugged. 'Well then, surely his papers will show that. That's the aim of the collection—to document what actually happened, not to twist anything, not to tamper with the facts.'

Mrs Vavasour smiled brightly as if Quinn had made a joke. For a few minutes she said nothing but used a poker to stir the fire vigorously. 'It may come as a surprise to you Mr Quinn, but what I'm burning aren't precious Nazi documents but personal letters addressed to Gerry when he lived in Kenya, and nearly all of them are from close friends of mine. You see, that's when Rex and I knew Gerry. And he was quite a chap.' She fished around in one of the wine cartons. 'Look, that's Gerald Despain—doesn't look much like a Nazi monster does he?'

She handed over a snapshot of a tall blonde man in white shorts and shirt and long white socks. The man was grinning widely, displaying large white teeth. Quinn stared at the photograph with a strange feeling of recognition: it was as if he knew the man or had seen him recently, looking just as he did in the picture, with a devil-may-care expression.

'And this was taken before the war—in Kenya?'

'Yes.' Mrs Vavasour snatched the photograph and stared hard at something on the back. '1938—in the Aberdare mountains.

Gerry's hey-day! Mine too, come to that. Oh yes, I'll admit that I was rather smitten—of course that was before I met Rex. Yes, dances at the club in 1938! Swing music! That vast expanse of sky! All those stars! Ah, happy days! Tell me, do you know anything at all about the Muthaiga Country Club Mr Quinn? No, I don't expect you do. Well, Jews were not allowed on the premises, and Gerry had nothing to do with that—he would have been at Eton when the rules were framed. So, you see, anti-Jewish feeling wasn't all that rare in those days.'

'Despain was a friend of your husband's too?'

'Oh yes, they were great chums, they often went shooting together. Gerry wasn't as good a shot as Rex, but Rex always said Gerry was a good bloke to have with you when you were after a lion. Quite fearless! He had a small plane, a Tiger Moth or something. Other friends of ours had a great barn at Burgeret, an open-ended affair, and someone dared Gerry to fly through it. Of course he did—practically gave Geraldine Soames a heart attack!'

'So are you going to destroy all the letters?'

'No, only some of the Kenyan ones. I'm keeping all those he received from Rex, every little scrap, may be useful for the biog. They'd known each other for years you see, ever since Eton. That's why I must read every word, in case any of the other letters mention Rex. And that's why I bought the collection. But I never expected any publicity. Oh sod that young reporter and his insinuations!'

Mrs Vavasour lapsed into silence. She lifted a tiny foot in a black high-heeled shoe, and looked speculatively at Quinn as if she might be coming to some new judgement about him. Quinn felt that his attitude to her was changing too. He felt sorry for her, leading a recluse-like life, embittered, brooding on the past and banking on a biography of her husband which the public might not appreciate. He asked her, 'Were you and your husband surprised when Despain went to Germany?'

'Surprised? That's hardly the word. Of course there was some delay before the news filtered through to Kenya. I don't think we heard that he was working for the Nazis till about '41 and by that time Rex was in England, with the RAF. But most people, including my family, thought Gerry must have gone quite mad, absolutely bonkers. I mean, not liking the chosen race over-much is one thing, but joining up with the ghastly Adolf Shicklgruber? No, definitely, surprised is not the word. Amazed, aghast! Of course he was always unpredictable, so full of energy, liable to go off pop. Mummy said that he was like a coiled spring. And Daddy never liked him, didn't trust him, something about the way Gerry treated the boys on his farm. Of course swearing at them was absolutely against Daddy's code of treating everyone fairly, he'd farmed in Kenya since 1919 you see. Well, I say, Mr Quinn, see what you've done, you've got me to say something against Gerry. Shall we have a drink?'

'Yes, please.'

'Just a tiny drop of gin for me. Most other things are there.'

Quinn walked over to the drinks trolley, studied the self-satisfied face of Rex Vavasour, MP, poured himself a small whisky and added a meagre amount of gin to Mrs Vavasour's glass.

Mrs Vavasour raised her glass when Quinn handed it to her. 'Well, cheers!'

I'm sorry you've drawn a blank with me and wasted a morning.'

'Not true. I've enjoyed the trip. Do you think I could see the German part of the collection even though there's no chance of your selling it?'

'I'm afraid not. But the only reason is that I don't have it or own it any longer. I gave it, d'you see, to Jumbo, my old friend General Erskine. From my point of view it was so much rubbish but he seemed to be interested. You could go and see him, tell him about your American customer. I have no idea how he would react, though I can't imagine that money would be much inducement to Jumbo.'

'Thank you. I may do that. You know what they say, where there's a will there's a way.'

'I'm prepared to believe it, Mr Quinn, though I've never put it to the test myself. Oh by the way, so that your morning is not a complete waste of time...' She bent down to search in another carton. 'Here, have this! It was left behind when we sorted out the stuff. Can't imagine that Jumbo will pine at not having it. So you can sell it to your customer and recoup your expenses.' She handed Quinn a small book in a red cloth binding with the title in black lettering set out aslant on the front cover:

THE
JEWS'
WHO'S
WHO

Quinn opened the red book right at the front. The endpapers were of thin yellow paper with engraved designs. On the first one there was an engraving of a ten-headed man with names set round the odd figure: 'Sir M Nathan, Mr Herbert Samuel, Sir E Cassel, Mr E S Montague, Sir Z Goschen, Sir A Mond, Earl Reading, Sir Edgar Speyer, Mr H S Samuel, Lord Rothschild,' with the inscriptions 'Privy Council' and 'Jewry Uber Alles'. The facing design was of a fat John Bull, with caricatured Jewish features, standing on a chest labelled 'Britain's Wealth'. By the side of this was a proclamation: 'Britons, our Country is dominated by Inter-national ALIEN financiers. INSIST on the act of settlement (1701) being restored and so prevent Britain being controlled by ALIENS.' 'Published by the "Britons",

175 Piccadilly, W.'

Quinn held the book up. 'Can I buy this from you? It must be rare and I shall only sell it.'

'No, Mr Quinn. I don't want the book and I don't need the money.'

He opened the book again, at the title-page where the publishers' name was alternatively given as 'The Judaic Publishing Co', with the date 1920. On it Gerald Despain had written his signature and inserted a small black bookplate with a monogram in silver: GWD. Mrs Vavasour saw that Quinn was studying the bookplate and explained, 'The W stood for Walters, his mother's maiden name. Gerry was mad about his mama. Often mentioned her though I can't remember his ever talking about his father, strangely enough. He always carried his mother's photograph and an old siver coin she had given him as a lucky piece.'

'Were you surprised when you heard that he had committed suicide?'

'Not at all. I should have thought it was inevitable once he was convinced that the Germans were beaten. He had too much spirit to bear being taken prisoner and put on trial! Besides, he never placed a great value on his life. You couldn't if you were willing to fly a plane through a barn. And he was always taking big risks, going off single-handed after a lion, that sort of thing.'

Quinn said, 'I must go. But thanks for the interesting talk, the drink and the book.'

Mrs Vavasour joined him as he started to walk out of the room. 'I've enjoyed meeing you Mr Quinn, but it's Jack isn't it?'

'Yes. So you have no objection to my contacting General Erskine?'

'None. He lives at a place called Nantyffin in Wales. When you phone Jumbo say straight out what your interest is. I've no idea whether he will see you but he likes straight talk. Operates by a strict code, like my father.'

'I'll do that.'

Mrs Vavasour waved her hand around in a vague gesture. 'I've rather let things go... After Rex died, I felt what is the point? But Jumbo says we must all continue to go forward. So I must do that.'

'Good.' Quinn reached out to shake her hand. 'Thanks again.'

'Goodbye Jack. Remember what I said about a biographer. Poor Rex!' Mrs

Vavasour made a despairing gesture towards her husband's portrait and Quinn sensed that she felt the biography might never be written.

CHAPTER 14

By the time Quinn had put his car in his garage in Bourdon Street and walked round to his office it was 5 pm. Instead of driving straight back to London he had gone on to Oxford for a pub lunch and a quick tour of the bookshops. As soon as he opened the door of 'Books International' he knew that June Whitall had had a tiring day of routine office work while he had been gallivanting round Oxfordshire. She had slightly astigmatic sight but wore her glasses only when her eyes were tired. She had them on but whipped them off as soon as he said, 'Hallo, girl Friday!' She had piles of books on either side of her typewriter and he could see that she had been cataloguing part of the large collection of poetry first editions he had bought in Cornwall. The pile of books with catalogue slips inserted was impressively large.

'Hallo. Not much biz today, as your friend Mr Dulau would say. Oh by the way, he popped in here just after lunch, looking rather handsome in a chocolate brown suit. Said to tell you he had identified the lady purchaser at the Mackmurdo sale as a Mrs Vavasour. He said she was reputed to be a millionairess—also that he was interested in the outcome of the Despain affair.'

'Oh is he? Well, that's for me to know and him to find out.'

'You're always very cagey about Mr Dulau.'

'I'm cagey! Let me tell you that Master Dulau is the world expert on caginess. I can't imagine him ever telling me the outcome of anything.' As Quinn said this he remembered Daniel remarking, 'You're like me Jack, you think that all knowledge is useful.'

June said, 'The post was late again today, you won't be surprised to hear. And it wasn't very interesting, but there were three cheques—one long overdue from Canada. Two letters from America were addressed to you personally so I left them on your desk. One is from

Mr Eckstein. Did you make any progress Despain-wise?'

'A little.' Quinn showed June the copy of *The Jews' Who's Who*. 'Mrs Vavasour gave me this. I offered to pay for it but she said no. I didn't feel too guilty as I suspected she was loaded. Her husband was an MP and I vaguely remember he was dropped from the Government over some big financial scandal. Lovely house!'

'What's she like?'

'You want a lightning sketch eh? Well, rather sad, embittered I would say. Lives alone in this big house, misses her husband who died in 1980, wonders what life's about without him, thinks he was wonderful and should be written about. Asked me to put her in touch with a biographer. Small, dark, with tiny feet—was attractive I should think—and very lively. Animated way of talking. Cat-lover and drinks too much, like me. I ended up liking her.'

'Oh you often do that. You expect not to like people and then you talk with them and change your mind.'

'Thank you Dr Freud. It's time you went home, June. You've done your stint for today.'

'I've still got this pile to finish.'

'I'll do those, prove that I can still catalogue books.'

'You're sure?' June asked doubtfully, but she started to do things preparatory to going home, putting her specs in their case and taking her tea-cup into the little room where there was a sink. As she emptied the tea-pot she asked, 'Will you be in tomorrow?'

'I hope not. What I mean is that I'm going to phone a General Erskine who has the Nazi material that will most interest Mr Eckstein. If he'll see me I shall probably go there tomorrow. He lives in Wales and I think the trip there and back will take up most of the day. Any special reason for asking?'

June emerged, wearing a red blazer over her dark blue frock. She said, 'Only that if you do go you'll miss Cyril Parkinson. He phoned up to say he will look in again tomorrow to brood over two books!'

'But with any luck I shall be in Nantyffin! I look forward to meeting the general. He sounds quite a guy, has five decorations including two for bravery in the last war. I can't imagine that he takes a favourable view of Gerald Despain.'

'You mean that Mrs Vavasour does?'

'Yes and no. She remembers him as a dashing handsome young man in Kenya, not as a Nazi supporter.'

'I hope you can arrange the trip to Wales. I'll make a fuss of Cyril Parkinson, give him two biscuits with his coffee.'

'Yes, do that. Goodbye June.'

June looked round the showroom to see that everything was in its place, then said goodbye. As Quinn listened to her footsteps down the hall he wondered for the hundredth time what he would do without her. He had a definite flair for buying books that were profitable but he had no talent for dealing with customers, and June largely carried the business, her talents complementing his own perfectly. She never complained that her salary did not compare with those earned by secretaries in thrusting London businesses or that the prospects of 'Books International' were not exactly bright. But then she never hinted at complaint about anything, and went home to Clapham every day to look after her aged mum.

A thought struck Quinn as he went into his own office and consulted his shelves of reference books. He searched the index of the *Greater London Atlas* but there was no Pickering Place listed, though there was a Pickering Avenue in the East End and a Pickering Street in North London. He was puzzled by this as Charlie Saunders had a phenomenal knowledge of London and was meticulous about such things as directions.

Quinn sat down at his desk and opened a letter from the Indiana University librarian saying that he would be glad to see an early copy of the catalogue of poetry they had in preparation; he then opened the one from Moishe Eckstein. Eckstein's letter was eccentrically typed on a quarto page with the Anna S Krugman Foundation heading, and had manuscript additions in black ink. At the top he had written in quotation marks: 'Hitler was a dark mirror held up to mankind'.

Dear Jack
POSTSCRIPT OR
SECOND THOUGHTS
ON G DESPAIN
I may be over-optimistic but the more I think about it the more hopeful I am that we shall obtain some of the Despain material. To me it seems unlikely that

another collector or librarian would want all three sections of the collection—the Eton & London letters; the East Africa material; the Nazi dossier. Obviously I am keenest about the Nazi papers and *particularly Despain's German diary* but don't turn down the chance of buying anything even though it is not of primary interest. All the material is of some interest in that it may give us a clue as to how/why this anti-Semite was formed. Did it happen when he was at school or in London? WHY? In Martin Gilbert's well researched book on the Holocaust which I am presently reading there is a crucial sentence: 'This is the greatest strength of the whole crime, its unbelievability.' Unbelievability applies to so much to do with the Nazis. Why should a wealthy young Britisher who spent much of his mature life farming in East Africa have become so infected with anti-Semitism that he was willing to forsake his friends and country and become a traitor? I look forward to hearing from you in due course.

Cordially,
Moishe

130

CHAPTER 15

Driving out of central London, heading for The Vale in Golders Green where Charlie and Lilian Saunders lived, Quinn felt low, his mood reflecting that of Lilian when he had phoned her. Lilian had said there was still no news of Charlie but she sounded very subdued as if she was convinced that something terrible had happened to him. Quinn could not accept this, but he realised that the period of silence must be frightening for Lilian whom he had known since he was a boy, calling her 'Auntie Lil'.

The route Quinn took he had taken a hundred times, and he drove round Regents Park and past Lords Cricket Ground as if on automatic, his mind busy with memories of Charlie over a thirty year period. Charlie had been the most regular trade caller at the second-hand shop which Quinn's father ran in Hammersmith. On occasion, when Quinn was still a schoolboy, Charlie would ask him if he fancied a Saturday morning trip out and take him to other, similar shops in what Charlie called 'the sticks', visiting London suburbs such as Ruislip, Harrow, Kenton and Stanmore. Quinn had learnt a lot from watching Charlie at the work he liked best, which was buying from other dealers, seeing him prowl round a shop mentally noting everything of interest but not indicating what he fancied until it was time for money to actually change hands. He had particularly enjoyed visiting such a shop in Harrow-on-the-Hill where the elderly proprietors Mr and Mrs Trumper sat in identical armchairs, with glum-looking faces, so close to the shop window that they looked as if they might be for sale. Charlie would joke about this while outside the shop but once inside would turn on the charm, paying adroit compliments and wheedling the generally unfriendly pair into parting with their choicest items at what Charlie called 'sensible prices'. Minutes later he would be driving down Harrow Hill, joking about 'Old Ma Trumper' whom he also called 'Mrs Punch'.

The traffic in Finchley Road was heavy, as usual, so that Quinn had to concentrate on his driving rather than memories of yesteryear, but as he turned off left into Dunstan Road he glanced right at West Heath Avenue which Charlie always said was *the* place to live in London, looking out on Golders Hill Park and Hampstead Heath, 'So you could have a nice walk before breakfast' he added, though he still limped from a war wound and did not care much for walking. He lived in a largely Jewish area, liked Jewish food and had Jewish taste in other things. Many of his friends were Jews. 'Always do business with Jews when you can,' he had urged Quinn on more than one occasion. 'They like business, they understand business. They're good at it and they are always willing to let the other fellow have a profit margin.'

As Quinn walked up the path to the Saunders' recently decorated house where the garden had its usual autumn display of chrysanthemums he could hardly believe that Charlie would not respond to the first ring of the bell, limping quickly down the hall, waving his arms about and calling out 'All right, already.'

Instead of Charlie's quick response there was silence even when he rang a second time. He imagined Lilian would be sitting in her kitchen with the wireless on. He used the heavy dolphin-shaped brass knocker. Wine-coloured glass in the top half of the door reflected a debased image of himself and he said aloud, as if the confession was jerked out of him, 'I'm not a patch on my old man.' Only the eyes in the wine-coloured portrait were authentic: the wary eyes of someone who expects that life will trick or disappoint him, whereas his father had always looked out tolerantly on the world, a man comfortable and at ease with his life.

Some moments after he knocked there were tripping steps in the hall and Lilian opened the door with a funny expression on her face, a sad attempt at a smile which reminded Quinn of Giuletta Massina in Fellini's film *La Strada*. She wore a mushroom-coloured frock; her hair looked more grey than blonde. Quinn took her in his arms and kissed her forehead. There was the familiar smell of lavender water. She felt hot as if she might have a fever but she shivered. A handkerchief was balled up in her left hand. She wasn't wearing her glasses and her grey-green eyes were glistening. She stepped back from his embrace and said, 'It's bad news, Jacky, I know it is. Even Sam knows.'

Quinn took hold of her hands. 'Now Lil. If you haven't heard anything then you can't *know* it's bad news. It's possible that Charlie's had an accident but very unlikely or you would have heard from the police. And Sam's a cat who is sensitive to all your moods, but he doesn't know anything. Where is he by the way?'

'Oh, hidden away somewhere. He's taken to hiding in the garden and he's sleeping on my bed at night, something he's never done before.'

'That's what I'm saying. Sam's very alert to how you feel. He's aware that you're upset and that worries him.'

Through a half-open door in the hall Quinn had a glimpse of the dining-room which contained too much furniture, like most rooms in the house. It looked unused, like a display area in a furniture department, and the curtains were partly closed, adding to an atmosphere of gloom.

Lilian Saunders sighed deeply and shrugged. She said, 'Come on through, Jacky, I've made some smoked salmon sandwiches. And there's a bottle of wine, or orange juice if you'd rather.'

135

Quinn said, 'I feel awful, Lil—about not remembering what happened on Friday night. I don't think I had masses to drink but I was taking two sorts of tablets and probably should not have been drinking at all...'

'You were certainly there with Charlie at the Sotheby's party. Lou Samuel saw you together. Lou said you both seemed to be enjoying yourselves, laughing together. Just—just like normal. And he thinks you went off together.'

'Well, I'm sorry Lil but my mind's still a blank—it makes me feel guilty but what can I do? And I'm sure I've never heard of Pickering Place which you said was mentioned in Charlie's diary...'

'There was something else I forgot to tell you when I phoned about the Sotheby's party. I'll show you in a minute,' Lilian said, leading the way into her large kitchen which was the only room downstairs to have a lived-in feel about it, furnished to her taste rather than housing items of Charlie's stock. The centre-piece of the room was a white Aga which she often praised. The kitchen table was covered with a duck-egg blue linen cloth and set for two with white plates and steel cutlery.

There was a bottle of Moselle in an antique wine-cooler, a dish of rye bread sandwiches and a jug of orange juice. Lilian looked out of the large window over the double sink and shook her head. 'You see, no sign of Sam. And this morning Mr Scott phoned, wanting to speak to Charlie. He was very surprised when I said Charlie must have gone off somewhere on business. You have to agree that it's odd he didn't say anything to Scotty either. Oh, just a sec, I'll pop upstairs, get something from Charlie's study.'

Quinn sat down at the table feeling perturbed about the telephone call from Frederick Scott. It was indeed strange that Charlie had not contacted him; Scott managed Charlie's antique shop in Neal Street and often figured in his conversations: 'Scotty's the ideal NCO, reliable, conscientious, and no ambition at all to set up in business for himself...' 'Scotty's an old woman, he'll never be a dealer if he lives to be a hundred! Why? Because he wants everything safe and sound. You and me Jacko, basically we're gamblers. We don't back horses but we backs our fancy.'

Quinn went to the window to see if he

could spy the cat. Under the window, on a tiled shelf, Lilian had arranged some of her favourite things: a photograph of Charlie as a young man with a full head of black hair, a china lamb, a snapshot of her niece as a baby, a paperweight of blue-green glass in which a sea-horse was immured.

Lilian came into the kitchen clutching a book to her chest. Under greyish-blonde hair her face was still youthful, but she had mottled old hands made lumpy by arthritis. She tried to manage a smile but did not succeed. 'To be honest Jacky I've been worrying quite a lot about Charlie recently. He's been very secretive lately and I know he didn't tell me the truth about a couple of phone calls. I don't mean he's been seeing another woman, I'm sure of that, but something's been going on. He's been very edgy, snappy—and you know that's not like him.'

'Now sit down Lil, have some wine, and try to stop worrying. Perhaps Charlie will turn up tomorrow and explain everything. It's possible he's been on edge about some big deal—you know how important business is to him.'

Lilian sat down as Quinn poured her a glass of wine. 'You may be right. That's what it's like being married to a man who boasts "I live to deal".'

Quinn poured himself a small amount of wine and added orange juice to it. 'What's the book?'

'Charlie's diary. When I told you he had written about you and the Sotheby's party on Friday I should also have said there was something about the next day—I was upset and not thinking straight.'

Lilian handed over the Boots Diary to Quinn who quickly found the entries she had mentioned. Charlie's writing was childish, large and easy to read: 'Sept 25th. Sotheby's party—ask Jacko about the Pickering Place party and meeting the terrible duo'. Underneath this enigmatic sentence he had made a brief entry for the 26th September: '2 to 3 am. Bill Shafto at Pin Mill.'

'Is there a place called Pin Mill in London, Jacky?'

Quinn shook his head. 'I've never heard of it, and out of the way places in London are a kind of hobby with me, Lil. No, I should say it's out of London. Are there any other references to Pin Mill in the diary? Perhaps he'd been there before?'

'But why should he go there between 2

and 3 am? Could it be a business meeting in the middle of the night?'

'I'll go through the diary and see what I can find out—if you like.'

'That's just what I wanted you to do Jacky. Charlie always said you would make a good detective. He said you'd got a nose for that kind of thing.'

'I'm interested in what makes people tick, that's what Charlie meant. Right, I'll take the diary with me and go through it carefully. And tomorrow, you must pop into the local police station, tell them that you are worried in case Charlie's been in a road accident, give them the registration of the BMW etcetera. Now will you do that?'

'I'll do it first thing, Jacky.' Lilian's face brightened a little. 'You are a comfort to me, dear.'

CHAPTER 16

After he had returned from seeing Lil Saunders, Quinn brewed himself some coffee—a mixture of Continental and Columbian beans, very strong, rich and aromatic. Strong coffee, olive oil and garlic were tastes of his which Madeleine did not share so that he had become competent at grinding coffee, making garlicky mayonnaise and an oily salad dressing. Looking round the kitchen of his Bourdon Street house Quinn thought of this in a bitter way for he was imagining a future in which he would be able to indulge these three tastes and go without all that he had in living with Madeleine and the girls. 'Serves you right—it couldn't happen to a nicer chap,' he said aloud as he poured himself a large mug of the rich brew.

Sitting down at the kitchen table he opened Charlie's diary at random and began quickly glancing through it with an odd mixture of feelings and memories. He had only glimpsed the diary on one occasion, but Charlie had referred to it as 'A complete record'. From what Charlie had said Quinn expected that it would list little of a personal nature but would record auction sales, prices paid for various items, appointments with other dealers and occasionally with customers though generally Charlie left the selling side of the business to Frederick Scott: 'Scotty can really *sell* things, something that you and I can't do, Jacko. We know why we want to buy things but we can't pass on the reasons. I always say too little or too much.'

After scanning a few pages of the diary it became clear that Charlie noted down his appointments in black ink and later added comments in red. On Thursday January 22nd 1987 he had attended a house sale near Leamington Spa and lunched nearby at a pub called The Green Man. In red ink Charlie afterwards commented that he had bid on a Queen Anne quarter-repeating bracket timepiece but had been unsuccessful, 'Outbid by Mallet.'

Like most dealers Charlie used a code for noting down his purchase prices: in his case the letters GREAT MINDS stood for the numbers 1 to 10, but this was idiosyncratically complicated by his use also of the letter X to stand for nought. As he often used this code conversationally, and would sometimes throw in a translation—'I'll give you RTX—£250'—most of his dealer friends knew the code. Once Quinn had bought an original drawing by 'Phiz' for *David Copperfield*, the one in which David made himself known to his Aunt Betsey. He had placed this on the wall of his office in Davies Street, unpriced since he was in no hurry to sell it. Charlie, on one of his rare visits to the Books International premises, had spied it immediately he entered the room and walked over to it saying, 'I like that—I like it, I want it and I'll give you AXX—£400.'

Quinn opened the diary at the first day in January and began to read it slowly, on the look-out for any references to Pickering Place, Pin Mill, Bill Shafto and 'the terrible duo'. He made his first discovery in the next month's pages and immediately solved the mystery of the place-name Pin Mill: 'February 1 Sunday To Pin Mill on the river Orwell. A12 as if going to Ipswick Airport then B 1456. Bill Shafto at 1 pm, "The Butt & Oyster".' In red ink Charlie had added the comment, 'Excellent pub. Shafto a young schemer but I like him and can do business with him. ETX a trip but this could be less sometimes when he does the same trip for "the terrible duo".'

On a sheet of typing paper Quinn wrote, 'Pin Mill in Suffolk near Ipswich. Shafto must own a boat, or more probably an aircraft as he charges £350 a trip.' Later in

February, on Sunday the 22nd, there was another diary reference to 'Pin Mill. Bill's boat WHY NOT? is a 1973 Huntsman with two 210 hp Sabre engines. Bill gave me the advert by which "the terrible duo" contacted him. An interesting day.' Pasted underneath his comment in red ink there was a small press cutting:

FLIGHT HEATHROW-ZURICH, Sunday, Oct 19 (BA 618 dep 18.30). Blonde, game for a laugh, wants to contact young, dark nautical type. You were reading a thriller and mentioned your boat Why Not? Please write Box 65 c/o Panache Publications, New Cavendish Street, London W1.

Quinn found three more references in the diary to Pin Mill but two of them were brief, just listing a time to be there with the red ink comment 'Satisfactory'. The red ink comment on a meeting at 'Pin Mill 2-3 am Sat 22 August' was more interesting: 'At last met "the terrible duo". An interesting couple, a right pair of chancers!'

Quinn closed the diary feeling pleased that he had got a definite lead on Pin Mill and Shafto. On an Ordnance Survey map of the Ipswich & The Naze area he found that Pin Mill was on the south bank of the River Orwell, close to the village of Woolverstone. He decided that if Charlie was still missing at the end of the week he would drive to Pin Mill and see if he could contact Bill Shafto, who seemed to make an exorbitant charge for a trip in his motor-boat.

CHAPTER 17

Nantyffin Lodge, near Crickhowell, was in a delightful situation, surrounded by a lush meadow sloping down to the River Usk. To the east there was a dramatic view of the Black Mountains. The house was at the end of a drive which led to the busy A40 road but it seemed secluded and quiet. When Quinn got out of his car he stood still for a few moments, enjoying the scene and taking stock of the long, low house which had a rose and madder facade. It was a perfect autumn day, the kind which Madeleine would have called 'halcyon', and the tops of the mountains were free of cloud. Everything about the General's house and garden was spick and span as if in contrast to Mrs Vavasour's—there was even an immaculate Union Jack fluttering from a freshly painted white pole.

The front door of the house stood open, disclosing a hallway lined with paintings and a tiled floor gleaming with polish. Quinn used a brass knocker finely modelled like a man's hand. As if in response to his knocking he heard a paroxysm of coughing followed by a drawn-out sigh. A moment later a man appeared, filling a doorway leading off from the hall. He was six foot four or five, with massive shoulders and the biggest hands Quinn had seen apart from those of a Negro heavyweight boxer. He had a comely mane of white hair stained at the front a kind of butterfly yellow. His eyebrows were black and dense. The set of his jaw would once have betokened insolence but there was a friendly look in his blue eyes. He wore a pullover of brown Shetland wool, a cream shirt open at the neck, Bedford cord trousers and highly polished brown boots. He smiled and said, 'Ah Quinn! I say, you're a man of your word! We said 2.30 and it's exactly 2.34.'

'I had very clear directions.'

'Easy enough so long as you spot the drive. You'd be surprised at how many people don't and find themselves halfway to Brecon.'

'What a lovely part of the world!'

'I expect you think it's an odd place to find a Scot but it was my wife's choice...' The General left the sentence hanging for a moment. His voice was unusually deep and Quinn could imagine him singing Mousorgsky's 'Song of the flea'. He inclined his big head towards the mountains: 'She loved that view. Of course you're seeing it at its best. We have more than our share of grey days. Well, do come in.'

As soon as he stepped into the hall Quinn's eyes were taken by an Archibald Thorburn painting of pheasants in flight, and he remembered Charlie Saunders confiding, 'They want Thorburn paintings of live birds.' Charlie always referred to collectors as 'They', somehow implying it was a race he found hard to fathom and harder still to pin down. Then Quinn noticed a fine Edward Lloyd oil of a gamekeeper picking up a dead magpie. He said, 'I like the Lloyd painting—super.'

'You deal in paintings as well as other things?'

'Not really, but you can't attend several hundred auction sales without some knowledge rubbing off.'

'Ah yes, of course. Come on through. You've had lunch?'

'In Crickhowell. Local salmon, very good it was too.'

'This way then. It's where I have the Despain material which Daphne—Mrs Vavasour—passed on to me. And the room in which I'm supposed to be writing my memoirs.' The General looked round at Quinn and grinned, momentarily transforming his face into a youthful version. 'Writing your memoirs covers a multitude of things, but mainly being sidetracked and staring out of the window. I'll tell you one thing Quinn, if you ever come to write your memoirs don't have a view like that.' He gestured towards a french window which was additionally framed at the left side by a magnolia tree and looked up to the mountains. 'And don't have a pair of sheepdogs who come round to the window and stare in at you beseechingly.'

Quinn glanced round the room two walls of which were book-lined, but his eyes rested on a dark photograph close to the door showing the General in a snow-covered field, surrounded by other soldiers who looked like pygmies by his side. The General followed his gaze and said, 'Holland, December '44. Probably you were in your pram then, but a low point in my war. A time of dilemma. I've thought of using it as an illustration in my book but there are so many possible captions: 'Monty says perhaps', 'Up against it' and 'Thank God for the Red Army'.

General Erskine sat down behind a desk on which books, a copy of the Mackmurdo sale catalogue, a ruler and papers were neatly arranged. Before he took a seat Quinn glimpsed a photograph of a lovely middle-aged woman with dark hair and eyes. In front of it there was a spotless green sheet of blotting-paper on which lay the red and gold packet of Dunhill International cigarettes, and one over-sized cigarette was placed parallel to the packet. Erskine picked it up, looked at it reflectively and said, 'Do you use these things? They say they can kill you.' He smiled in a strange way and Quinn had a very strong intuitive feeling that the verdict was already in on the General and that was the reason for the violent coughing which had punctuated their early morning phone call. He could not justify that feeling but he had learnt to trust his intuitions.

'No thanks, I don't smoke.'

'Very wise.' The General smiled again as his carefully manicured fingers played with the cigarette. 'Well, there are the Despain papers, etcetera.' He used his right boot to indicate four wine cartons which stood near the desk. 'Daphne told me that your interest is a commercial one—that you have an American client who will pay a premium to obtain them.'

'That's true and I'm here really on his behalf, but I must say I've begun to be interested in Gerald Despain myself. Mrs Vavasour...'

'Oh I expect Daphne had you half convinced that Gerry was a much mis-understood man and that he ended up in Germany largely by mistake. Not true of course. I tell you what, Quinn, you won't hear me say much in favour of Despain but one had to admit that it must have taken a lot of courage, of a queer kind but nonetheless, to fly to Germany in '39. Just imagine landing there and trying to explain what you were up to with only a couple of pamphlets to bolster your credentials. But no-one could say Gerry lacked guts.'

'You first met him at Eton?'

'Oh no, he was nine years older than me. I only knew him for a few months in '38. I had a longish stretch of sick-leave then and spent it with my brother who farmed in Kenya. Gerry was supposed to be farming too but he didn't keep his nose to the grindstone like my brother—any excuse and he was off shooting or flying his plane. I'll admit I was rather impressed by him at first but when you're young you're liable to be impressed for the wrong reasons. And he was rather a dashing fellow, very physical, with movements that were a touch theatrical. He was much given to vaulting—finishing off a game of tennis with a volley drive and then over the net! Jaunty, now there's a word that's gone out of fashion, and devil-may-care. But finally I got the impression that he didn't give a bugger for anyone. Daphne's father felt the same and he was a good judge of men.'

'Did his anti-Semitism impinge on you?'

'Not on me, but it obviously started much earlier than the nineteen-thirties...' Erskine ferreted about in one of the cartons. 'I can't lay my hands on it at the moment but somewhere there you will find copies of a scurrilous anti-Jewish rag called the *Imperialist* which came out during the first World War. So he must have subscribed to that circa 1918. Now there's a rarity for your client!'

'So you will sell the collection?'

'Not at the moment because I'm enjoying playing about with it, and there's always a chance I may come across something useful for my book. Give me another month and I shall have finished with it. We'll make an appointment for early in November. You'll come down then and have a lunch cooked by my Mrs Davies. You will make me a generous offer and give me a cheque made out to a charity I shall designate. Your persistence will be rewarded and your client should be happy.'

'I'm sure Mr Eckstein will be delighted. He's making the collection to help people try to understand what happened. It's a rather specialised collection because he's concentrating on books and papers relating to anti-Semites of various countries who joined the Nazi cause or sympathised with it.'

'Then perhaps he'll be interested in a tale about Despain when he was at his first school. It was a rather unusual place called Durnford School at Langton Maltravers on the Dorset coast—small, but much favoured in the Edwardian epoch for boys destined for Eton, run by a somewhat eccentric man called Tom Pellatt. That writer fellow Ian Fleming went to Durnford about that time. The story I heard was that Benjamin Despain visited the school to see Gerald when he was seven or eight. Afterwards a caricature of Benjamin, a beard-and-hooked-nose kind of thing, appeared on a black-board, with the inscription "Despain is a Yid". That must have bitten deep.'

'It must indeed. Mrs Vavasour told me that Despain was proud of taking after his mother, a statuesque blonde type apparently.'

'Yes, she was. Gerry once showed me her photograph, just the kind of blonde that Hitler was obsessed with. By the way...' General Erskine stopped talking as he searched among various items in one of the cartons. 'Speaking of that evil genius—here's a photograph of the Bohemian Corporal which makes him look as if butter wouldn't melt in his mouth.' The General laughed and his laughter caught on some phlegm and he began to cough. He coughed so much that his face became red and he could not speak; his face contused, silently he handed a photograph over to Quinn. The snapshot showed Hitler, dressed in a longish grey jacket and black trousers, smiling and bending down to pat an Alsatian dog.

Quinn studied the photograph intently while Erskine recovered from the bout of coughing. When it was over the General picked up some more photographs and shuffled them like a pack of cards. Some he held aloft as he said, 'And what am I bid for these pretty things? I warn you Quinn I shall expect a good offer. I want it so that my charity at least will benefit from Despain's treachery. You see, here we have Hitler's great favourites, Eva and Gretl Braun, and here's Heinrich Hoffman, Hitler's court photographer. Also Richard Gehlen, the legendary Nazi intelligence officer, General Koller, ah and yes, here is Gerry's German wife when she was still Fraulein Herta Schellenberg. Yet another strapping blonde beauty.'

The General picked up a pen and held it like a cigarette before pointing it at some photographs on the wall. 'Incredible the amount of misery that Bohemian Corporal brought into this world! You know, Quinn, the more I think about it the more I'm convinced that these things should go into Mr Eckstein's collection. But one thing—no publicity of any kind—I don't want a newspaper printing some small item that makes me out to be a profiteer. Our transaction is to be strictly confidential, that's understood?'

'Of course. Mr Eckstein's not looking for any publicity himself.'

'Good. Daphne was very upset because some reporter found out she had bought the collection...' The General laughed. 'I know—of course—the fat man at Marlow—that very devious looking fellow, he must have sold them Daphne's address.' Erskine looked at Quinn for confirmation of his theory but it was not forthcoming. 'So you're saying nothing. Well, good, you can tell your client that the Despain deal

155

is on—subject to a satisfactory offer in November.'

Quinn said, 'I look forward to it. Do you think I could see Despain's German diary?'

'I'm afraid not, for the simple reason that I don't have it—Daphne gave it to our companion at the sale. I'm not going to try to keep his identity a secret as you seem so adept at tracking people down. Gerald Despain's nephew, the Hon Toby Walters, has the diary. But don't contact him until I've had a word with Toby myself—see how he feels about it. Now I shall rely on that. And you can rely on me phoning Toby and telling him of your interest.'

General Erskine stood up and looked down on the four cartons, suddenly lost in thought. He was an impressive figure, brooding and monitory. Quinn could understand that bleak mid-winter scene in Holland in 1944 when soldiers had hung upon his words, and how Mrs Vavasour had taken his advice. 'We must all continue to go forward.' Erskine shook his head. 'Strange. It's forty-two years since Gerry blew his brains out yet he's still causing some kind of disturbance... That's what he did you know, shot his wife while she was sleeping, then stuck a big Mauser pistol in his mouth. Left a note blaming the war on International Jewry... Ah well, life goes on Quinn. Now I'm going to leave you alone to look through this stuff at your own pace, without me hovering over your shoulder. I must take the dogs for a walk. When I come back I'll organise some tea. I understand that Mrs Davies has made one of her celebrated banana cakes. Enjoy yourself—I think you'll find it interesting.'

CHAPTER 18

After his trip to Wales Quinn did not feel like cooking so he decided on a picnic supper of Cheshire cheese, nectarines, white seedless grapes and Bulgarian Cabernet Sauvignon. He put these things on his kitchen table, poured out a tumbler of wine and sipped it, then felt restless and began pacing about like a caged lion. The prospect of an evening by himself was daunting yet he did not feel like going out. 'A concert at home,' he said aloud. Music would make him feel more relaxed and would help pass the time. A Mozart and Gershwin concert beginning with Mozart's Sinfonia Concertante played by Perlman and Zukerman; then some Gershwin songs, Mozart's Clarinet Quintet, Gershwin's Piano Concerto...

Planning this music programme Quinn walked into his living-room, mentally agreeing with his daughters that it did look a mess and a new carpet was the number one priority. He hovered over a carton containing records and found the Mozart Concertante. The moment it was revolving on his record player he felt better able to relax. Mozart, as usual, had a magical effect. 'Music is God's way of trying to communicate with us,' he said aloud. In the empty flat his voice sounded loud and pompous but the idea, if original, seemed worth recording. It did not fit in with his other epigrams such as 'I'm underwhelmed by people's generosity', and seemed more profound than his usual ideas so he decided to write it down, but the front door bell rang interrupting his thoughts. He glanced at his watch and saw that it was 8.30 pm—too late for the caller to be one of his daughters. An evening caller at his

Bourdon Street house was such a rarity that he thought it might be Charlie Saunders to explain his disappearance act, or Madeleine to talk things over. He ran down the stairs and opened the door to be confronted by an attractive woman in her late thirties. She was short, perhaps five feet one or two, with a mass of reddish-gold hair piled up on top of her head, a tip-tilted nose and large, downward-slanting brown eyes. She was the woman at whom he had been staring at the party when his blonde companion had said, 'If I read your mind right, Mr Jeremy Fisher, I expect you think all her zones would be erogenous.'

She said in a surprisingly deep voice, 'It's true, you see, the mountain does sometimes come to visit Mahomet.'

Quinn said, 'Grand! How nice! Come in.'

The woman stayed where she was, smiling at him. 'What a joke, you don't remember me, do you? Anna Campaspe. We met at that weird party on Friday night. You gave me a card with your home and business addresses. I was going to give you my phone number but we were interrupted. Well, Jack Quinn, what to do?'

'Please come in. I do remember you, I

remember looking at you across the room. If I seem vague it's because everything about that party is vague and muddled up in my mind. I had much too much to drink...'

'Like many of the guests. Champagne was being handed round like water...' Anna stopped talking but still made no move to enter the house. Her eyes were heavily made up but there was no lipstick on her mouth. She wore a dress of lavender cotton with violet coloured shoes. Quinn put out his hand towards her. 'I did want to see you again. I don't know why I didn't take your number but I wish I had.'

Anna said 'Oh yes?' doubtfully, giving him a guarded look.

'You have my word for it.'

'It's understood between us that I would not have come here...'

Quinn took her arm and pulled her gently over the threshold, saying, 'Believe me, it's the high point of my day. Come upstairs and have a glass of wine.'

'Well, yes, thank you.' Anna entered further into the tiny hall and stepped past Quinn to climb the stairs. He could smell a heady mixture of scents. Her hair was alive with light and movement. As she mounted the first steps an image of red tendrils of hair on a white neck was imprinted on his brain. He noticed that she had narrow white hands covered in freckles. He felt excited and intrigued. She ran up the stairs then spun round to look at him again, closely as if trying to read his mind. He wondered how much of her manner was mockery.

'I like this house—and the quiet street. A sort of secret place which I'll never be able to find again, like the mysterious Grand Meaulnes in that French book.' She entered the kitchen and ran over to the window to look out. 'Quite definitely an up-market street.'

Quinn said, 'Don't be fooled by the house. I could never afford to buy it, and I'm only renting it because I got a cheap tail-end lease, just two years...'

'Any other drawbacks I should hear about?'

'Any number. But have some wine and then they may not seem so bad.'

'I see I've interrupted your supper.'

'It's the kind that's easily shared. Have something.'

Anna reached out with her left hand to break off a piece of cheese and Quinn saw that she wore a wide gold wedding ring. He poured her a tumbler of wine. When she took it she stood provocatively close to him, smiling and saying nothing. Her luxuriant hair had a fresh herbal scent. She touched her glass to his and said, 'So let's hear more about your drawbacks. The fact that you can't afford this house but are living in it sounds more like a bonus to me.'

'The other drawbacks are more serious, more permanent. I'm too impulsive, I'm always doing things without thinking them through, I never read the small print, I rush in where wise men fear to tread.'

'A victim of your own temperament.'

'Something like that. I've been told so often enough.'

'Well, tell me something positive. What do you like?'

'Women, children, music, books, wine.'

'Ah, all the right priorities.'

'Why did you call that party weird?'

'It was very strange because hardly anybody seemed to know the host. I didn't meet him. And where did you disappear to? One moment I saw you arguing with a smallish chap a good deal older than you—the next moment you'd vanished.'

As Anna said this Quinn did remember arguing with Charlie Saunders, and that he had been worried by Charlie's tense nervousness, something that was quite out of character. He said, 'This is also going to sound weird—where was the party? You see I went there with a friend and I blotted right out at the end.'

'Somewhere off St James's Street. I can't be more exact than that as I also went there with a friend, in a taxi, but I know the taxi stopped in St James's and that we walked through a narrow alleyway to some flats.'

'Well, that's a clue. It's very frustrating having this blank period in my life. But I do remember staring at you across the room.'

'I can fill in a bit of the blank because you were standing next to my friend at the time, chatting her up. I saw you put your arm round her waist.'

'A tall blonde with a Botticelli face?'

'That's right, yes, she's tall and blonde. Tamsin Guild. But you don't remember what you were saying to her?'

'Not a word. I just remember her looking round at people and saying, "Brief lives, brief lives".'

'Ah, that's Tamsin all right. She has this very cynical attitude to life. Says it's all a swindle, a cruel hoax.'

'Why's that?'

'Hard to say. I've known her ever since we were at school together in Cheltenham, but I don't pretend to understand her. She had a miserable childhood because both her parents were killed in a car crash when she was small. She was brought up by an aunt—without much affection I think.'

'She called me Mr Jeremy Fisher.'

'Well, don't be put out by that. She sometimes calls me Mrs Tiggy Winkle. She only uses those Beatrix Potter names with people she's interested in.'

'And I think someone called her Tommy.'

'Ah yes, that would be her friend Tom, the mysterious glamorous Tom, he calls her that. Tom and Tommy you see. He's the reason I see Tamsin so rarely—they lead a very glamorous life, always travelling, Paris, Athens, Cairo, New York.'

'So they don't live in London?'

'No, so your chances of seeing her again are slim. Tamsin tells me that they have a base on some obscure Greek island, Kos or Ixos or somewhere like that. "Somewhere to rest and recuperate," she says. Typical

Tom and Tommy stuff. Why did you say that she had a Botticelli face?'

'I can show you exactly what I mean. This way.' Quinn indicated the doorway opening on to the passage leading to his bedroom. He put down his glass and she followed suit. She raised her eyebrows and smiled. He felt that she was the kind of woman who took going to bed for granted and knew more about it than he did in his wildest dreams.

Anna said, 'So the proof about the Botticelli face happens to be in your bedroom! How very convenient if Tamsin decides to call on you. Don't tell me you own a Botticelli and can't afford to rent this house.'

'Only three reproductions, but they're beautiful and worth seeing.'

'Right, lead on. By the way, what's the music?'

'Mozart.'

'Mm—Mozart and Botticelli! Nothing but the best in Bourdon Street.'

As Anna followed Quinn into the bedroom she was humming a little tune that had nothing to do with Mozart. Moments later he recognised it as the song 'Let it be me'.

Quinn pointed to the painting above his bed, saying, 'I meant that your friend Tamsin has a face rather like Botticelli's Venus.'

'Yes, very strategically placed.' Anna clambered on to the bed to peer myopically at the painting, displaying quite a lot of shapely leg. Quinn put his right hand on the back of her left knee. Anna said, 'I see what you mean but it appears that Botticelli thought Venus was a redhead.'

'More wine?' Quinn asked.

'Definitely more wine.'

When they were back in the the kitchen and their glasses had been refilled they stood close together sipping the wine and looking at each other. Anna studied Quinn closely as if looking for faults, so that he felt like a grandfather clock being scrutinised by Charlie Saunders.

Anna said, 'So what happened after you left the party? I turned round to take a glass of champagne and you had vanished.'

'I can't tell you much. It appears that I fell down in the street, hitting my head. A policeman saw me and had me whisked off to hospital. I woke up during the night and found I was in the casualty ward. It's an experience I don't want to repeat.'

'I cursed that vanishing trick of yours—I fancied you something rotten then. There you were at this smart party, big and burly, with your tie askew and hair rumpled, looking as if you didn't give a damn about anything. A modern MacHeath! Someone who wouldn't take no for an answer.'

'Wrong, I'm afraid. Don't be fooled by the broken nose. Nowadays I quite often take no for an answer. I only sensed a no from Tamsin, and that was enough.'

'Ah well, Tamsin only has eyes for the wonderful Tom who leads a charmed life according to her.'

Anna's voice was deep and husky like Greta Garbo's. Quinn liked it and her unpainted mouth, and her large down-slanting eyes in which the pupils seemed to change size. They both put down their glasses. When he opened his arms Anna came into them as if she had been doing so for years. She said, 'Kiss me,' and her kiss was sweet and drugging. Quinn was immediately aroused and knew there would be no sexual fiasco with her. Hugging her he lifted her off her feet and carried her out of the kitchen. As he walked towards the bedroom she said his name twice and then whispered, 'Darling'.

★ ★ ★ ★

Quinn woke from a confused dream in which he had been standing in a street arguing with Charlie Saunders. Arguing badly because he was in an alcoholic daze so that he could not think straight or put forward his point of view sensibly. He had been trying to persuade Charlie not to do something, perturbed at seeing that Charlie was worried and plainly nervous, quite unlike his usual self. Quinn came slowly out of the dream, face down in the pillow. Traces of perfume reminded him of Anna's presence and he reached out for her with his left hand, finding nothing to touch but disturbed sheets and an empty pillow. Anna's absence jerked him properly awake and he lifted his head to look around at the vacant room and open door. He switched on the bedside lamp and sprang from the bed, mystified. For a moment it seemed to him that Anna might have been part of an earlier dream but in the bed there was visible evidence of her presence in smudges of eyeliner on the pillows. Naked he walked out into the passage, hoping she might be in the lavatory or bathroom, but both rooms had open doors. Feeling foolish he called out her name, then walked into the kitchen. When he turned on the light he saw that a piece of paper had been propped up against the bowl of fruit. There was a pencilled note in large, pointed, excitable writing:

Darling MacHeath

Sorry I had to scoot but I was supposed to be somewhere else if you know what I mean... But I'm sure you will understand. 'Oh what a tangled web we weave when first we practice to deceive.' Sorry! But I shall be knocking on your door again and, hopefully, shall be able to stay longer...

I wanted to see you again, and I'm glad I was bold enough to call, but I should tell you that Tamsin asked me to find out what happened to you last Friday night! I wonder why? Perhaps she's more interested in Mr Jeremy Fisher than you thought... Can't tell you how to find her as we've only been in touch by phone and we met up on Friday in a pub in New Cavendish Street. Besides I want to keep you from her. I loved lying in your arms beneath the benign stare of Botticelli's Venus.

Love from Anna

CHAPTER 19

Soon after 9 am on Thursday mornings it was June Whitall's custom to leave the Books International premises and walk to New Bond Street to bank the cheques received by the firm during the week and do any errands she considered necessary.When she set out on October 1st she said she would probably be away about an hour as she was going to stock up on envelopes, etcetera. Quinn settled down to write a letter to Moishe Eckstein reporting on the progress he had made with regard to the Despain papers. Using her electric typewriter June could produce a faultless letter looking as if it had been printed, but Quinn preferred to do his own typing when writing to Eckstein and a few other customers whom he had come to regard as friends. He inserted a foolscap letter-heading in his old Olympia machine and began to type quickly because the letter was already partly written in his head:

Dear Moishe,
Interim report on Gerald Despain
The collection of Despain papers sold by Messrs Younger in Marlow was the property of a dead man, a Major Adrian Mackmurdo who served with the British Army in Germany in 1944/5. Mackmurdo obviously obtained the Despain collection, and a good many other things included in the Marlow sale, during his service there, so the provenance of such papers, books, engravings & paintings is rather doubtful. Apparently this point was discussed by some of the dealers at the sale. As it all happened over forty years ago who can say whether Mackmurdo had a good title to the items? He may have bought them or possibly he 'liberated' (ie just took) them. I can't see there will be any problem over this but I think I should mention it to you.

The name 'Principle' given for the buyer at the Marlow auction was just a cover for a Mrs Daphne Vavasour (the widow of a Conservative MP, Rex Vavasour, who once held a position in the Government here). Mrs Vavasour lived in Kenya when she was a young woman and knew Despain while he was there, and that was the reason she bought the collection because she wanted to go through the East African section. She is keeping any letters from her husband and any that relate to him as she has the idea of a biography being written of Rex Vavasour; she is destroying the other Kenyan letters. I understand she is a very wealthy woman and would not have been interested in any financial offer we could have made, so you will have to forget that section of the collection. She did give me one book which I'm sure must be rare and it bears Despain's bookplate (probably printed in Germany). Details below.

Mrs Vavasour had two companions at the sale and one of them, the Hon Toby Walters who is Gerald Despain's nephew, has the German diary you particularly wanted. I expect I shall be put in touch with Walters and will see what I can do there.

The rest of the material was given to the other person at the auction with Mrs Vavasour, a General James Hugh Erskine who lives in Wales. I have been to see Erskine and am hopeful that in about a month's time I shall be able to purchase the stuff that he owns. Once again he is wealthy and not liable to be tempted in that way, but he seems quite keen on the Despain material bringing in a sizable cheque for his favourite charity.

General Erskine allowed me to spend two hours in going through the collection and I think you will find it of great interest. Apparently Mackmurdo—who found the papers in Hamburg—did some research on Despain, also on the autocratic Walters family who provided a wife for Benjamin Despain. Both Mackmurdo and Ralph Younger who catalogued the material for the Marlow sale, took a dislike to Gerald Despain. I must say I agree with their judgement as I too have come to dislike him—just the kind of swaggering bully to fit into the Nazi band.

In my opinion the 'letters 1940–1945' are *not* of great interest, from your viewpoint, being rather routine and quite adequately described in the Younger catalogue. It is the material of the 1920s which I think will fascinate you. Apparently while Despain was in his last year at Eton he subscribed to a curious newspaper, first called *The Imperialist* and then *The Vigilante,* published in 1918. This paper was published to spread the reactionary right-wing ideas of the proprietor, an eccentric MP called Noel Pemberton-Billing. He had found a number of like-minded contributors, including a Captain Spencer who had been dismissed from the British Secret Service as being insane, a sinister Dr J H Clarke who specialised in racial hatred, and H H Beamish who was violently anti-Semitic. Despain was in touch with all these men and wrote an article 'The Unholy Empire' for *The Vigilante.* Some fascinating letters in this correspondence, showing how unhinged the whole bunch were. Two years later Despain was also friendly with an equally unpleasant crowd called 'The Britons', then to be found at 175 Piccadilly, London, who published THE JEWS' WHO'S WHO, listed below.

Quinn paused to read his letter to see if he should add any more. When he was halfway through it his telephone rang. He answered by simply saying 'Quinn' because he could never bring himself to say 'Books International' which tripped off June's tongue so easily and impressively, as if the business really was a big organisation. There was a pause so he repeated his name, then he heard Lilian Saunders saying, 'Jacky, is it you Jacky?'

'Yes, hello Lil. Any news of Charlie?'

'No dear, nothing, not a word. I went round to the Police, like you told me, and they made a note of his name and the car's registration number and said they would ring me immediately if they heard anything. The sergeant said there wasn't much else they could do at present and that it was early days yet. I suppose it is from their point of view, but I'm very worried.'

'I know you are, Lil. I shall be home this evening so phone me there if Charlie suddenly turns up. If you don't phone then I shall go to that place called Pin Mill. It's near Ipswich and I'll drive there tomorrow morning and have a word with a chap called Bill Shafto if I can find him. It said in Charlie's diary that Shafto owns a boat so I suppose there's a chance that Charlie went off with him somewhere. Anyway I'll find out what I can.'

'Thanks dear. Perhaps Mr Shafto will tell you something...'

'I think it's possible, Lil. Anyway it's the best lead we have, so leave it to me.'

'I will dear, I am grateful.'

'Nonsense, I want to do it.'

'Goodbye, Jacky.'

Jumbled thoughts and memories of Charlie Saunders filled Quinn's mind momentarily so that he could not concentrate on the letter to Eckstein. He went to the window and looked down the street to the towering tree in front of Mallet's house on the corner of Bourdon Street—Mallet was the only antiques firm that Charlie envied and he would often comment on their superb premises. In Quinn's mind there was a panicky fear that perhaps Charlie had been involved in a tragic accident, possibly in Shafto's boat, and he subdued it by thinking hard about his unfinished letter then suddenly remembering he had not asked Lilian Saunders to check whether Charlie's passport was missing.

He drank up the remainder of the coffee June had made and began typing again:

Despain's two anti-Semitic pamphlets THE JEWISH OCTOPUS and A STUDY IN GREED were both privately printed but it seems probable that they were distributed by the group called 'The Britons'.

By the way, you will be interested to hear that Gerald Despain was cashiered from the Punjab Rifles in 1923 for striking an Indian soldier with a stick. He really was all of a piece!

Best wishes

Quinn signed the letter, then re-inserted it in the machine to add a postscript:

We can quote: THE JEWS' WHO'S WHO. Anonymous, dated 1920 and the publisher's name given as 'The Judaic Publishing Co'; also 'Published by the "Britons", 175 Piccadilly, W.' Original red cloth with black lettering; pale yellow endpapers with caricatured Jewish features. Slight signs of wear on the original cloth binding, otherwise a very good copy. Rare. With Gerald

Despain's signature in ink and his black
& silver bookplate, 'GWD'.

£50

The telephone rang as Quinn folded up
the foolscap page, and there was a pause
after he said his name. He thought it might
be Lilian Saunders again and reminded
himself to ask her about Charlie's passport,
but a moment later he heard a male
Cockney voice, talking quickly.

'Mr Quinn. This is Fred Scott, Charlie's
manager. I've just been talking to Mrs
Saunders and I need to see you urgently.
It's important. Can we meet this morning?'

'Sure, Fred. Do you want me to come
to the shop or could you pop round to
Davies Street?'

'I'd be grateful if you could meet me
somewhere else, it's a very confidential
matter. Concerns Charlie, you see. Do you
know St Paul's Church, just off Henrietta
Street? Could you meet me there in half
an hour, say?'

'You mean the actors' church? Yes, I
can see you there. Half an hour will be
okay.'

'Well, thanks very much.' Scott sounded
relieved, as if he had thought that

178

Quinn might not be willing to follow his instructions. 'That's a load off my mind, I'm grateful, very grateful. Goodbye now.'

CHAPTER 20

Walking briskly along Maddox Street, Quinn found that he was whistling the tune of 'Let it be me'. Immediately he thought of Anna Campaspe's large eyes circled in black, her luxuriant hair and kitten-like face, wondering if he would ever see her again. He brooded on this for a minute or two, then decided he had no idea. It was strange to make love to a woman and have her go off to sleep in your arms and know so little about her: all he knew was her friendship with Tamsin Guild and her name which might be fictitious. But there was nothing he could do about the unsatisfactory situation—it was obvious that she was married so it would be unfair to track her down through the telephone directory. He managed to put her out of his mind by concentrating on his forthcoming meeting with Frederick Scott.

Quinn had done the walk from his office in Davies Street to Charlie's shop so often that he thought he could do it blindfold. He followed the same route in going to St Paul's Church in Covent Garden as it was the quickest way, and he felt impelled to glance at Charlie's shop even though Scott had chosen not to see him there. He took a series of short streets running parallel to Oxford Street, through the bustling Soho area he liked and where he had most frequently met Charlie for lunch. They had, over a twenty-year period, occasionally gone further afield to The Kosher Luncheon Club in Greatorex Street, to Bloom's in Whitechapel High Street and The Stage Door in Thayer Street, but their favourite venue was Siegel's in Berwick Street. Charlie preferred Jewish food and Quinn was happy to go along with that preference though he chose Greek or Italian cuisine when he lunched alone. It was in Jewish restaurants, usually over a plate of salt beef or pastrami, that Charlie had continued Quinn's education as a dealer. Quinn could still remember precepts he had been given in the early days: 'Bank your cheques, deal with your orders, deal with your letters, deal with enquiries'; 'Never expect something for nothing'; 'If it was easy, Jacko, everyone would be doing it'; 'The secret is in the buying'.

When Quinn passed the corner of Broadwick Street and Berwick Street he half expected to encounter Charlie limping along hurriedly, grinning, a knowing look in his eye, full of enthusiasm and with half-a-dozen stories to tell in Siegel's crowded restaurant where everybody seemed to know everybody and the rooms buzzed with loud, excited voices.

Walking down Wardour Street Quinn was puzzling over why Scott should choose to meet at St Paul's Church, and wondering why he obviously did not want their conversation to be overheard even by the two other people who worked in Charlie's shop—Mrs Thompson, a pleasant middle-aged woman, and Sidney Jackson, a tall youth who did most of the hard physical work necessary to run a thriving antiques business. Though he had seen Scott scores of times in visiting the shop, Quinn could not remember a single occasion when they had done more than swap pleasantries. Scott had a moon-shaped face, thick glasses and an invariably serious expression. His seriousness and air of probity were characteristics that Charlies stressed in talking about him: 'Course, Scotty's not only one hundred per cent honest but he looks it. Everybody trusts him and thinks he's wiser than he is. That big forehead and the thick glasses. You know I don't think he *could* tell a lie, Jacko, not like you and me. Christ! he's so honest it's painful sometimes. I'm sure he worries about whether I'm paying enough tax. And VAT? He's got VAT on the brain! I had to tell him, look Scotty, I said, it's me what pays your wages, not the bloody VAT man.'

Charlie Saunders had a shop at the end of Neal Street which joins Shaftesbury Avenue; he had acquired it in 1970 on a cheap twenty-year lease and was indifferent or hostile to the changes which had taken place in the area since that time. 'Why do they have to change everything?' he complained. 'I liked the old Garden, a genuine part of working London, everyone bustling about trying to make a crust. What you got today? Streets full of kids with nothing to do but watch the buskers. That's an improvement?' Nor had he welcomed the fact that Neal Street had been made into a pedestrian way: 'I don't want passing trade. Lot of time wasters! The pot lid brigade! Bargain hunters! What I need I had the day I signed the lease—large premises within a taxi ride of the good hotels. I don't want a shop full of people killing time at my expense.'

Quinn stood still at the top of Neal Street and surveyed Charlie's shop which had a facade painted dark blue with a single word in gold: ANTIQUES. There were just three items in the shop window because it was Charlie's policy to show only a few highly priced items to scare off bargain hunters. One was a superb grandfather clock, identified on a neat sales ticket: 'An 1820 silvered-dial striking clock by the London maker William Vale—£6,500'. There was also a ladderback armchair designed by Charles Rennie Mackintosh, and a large gold watch in a gold case. The sale ticket for the watch had been awkwardly placed so that Quinn had to crouch to discover that it had been made in 1790 by William Carpenter. It was in this awkward posture that he saw Mrs Thompson standing inside the shop and exchanged a conspiratorial smile. Quinn waved to her, then walked off in case she should come to the door.

Hurrying down Neal Street towards the Covent Garden tube station, Quinn felt that Frederick Scott was overdoing the cloak-and-dagger business by arranging their meeting at the church. Charlie's shop was large and had a cellar—it would have been easy to find a private place for their talk. Then it struck him that there might be something not quite above-board about Charlie's disappearance which had driven Scott to request the unusual assignation. Charlie had once said, 'I never mention anything a bit dodgy to Scotty. Christ! He would have kittens!'

St Paul's Church, Covent Garden, was placed so that an entry into the grounds could be made through three streets. Choosing the one in Henrietta Street, Quinn saw that the area in front of the church was empty despite it being a fine sunny day. He took a seat beneath a tall graceful tree and stared at the handsome portico where Professor Higgins and Eliza Doolittle had met in 'My Fair Lady'. Well, Scotty, Quinn thought, this should be private enough for you to blurt out that Charlie's been fiddling his taxes as well as bunking off.

Quinn felt alert, slightly tense, more than usual on his guard; something to do with the encounter with Anna Campaspe in which he felt that he had not been told the truth. He was very critical of himself and had no illusions about his looks, tending to agree with the bookseller he had once overheard describing him as 'looking like an Irish navvy'. That being the case, was it likely that Anna Campaspe would have fancied him on sight? He wished there was some magical draught he could take to clear his mind about the mysterious party on Friday night but as he tried again to concentrate on it he spotted Frederick Scott approaching through the Inigo Place entrance in Bedford Street. Scott walked with a fast mechanical gait, plunged in thought, oblivious of his surroundings. Quinn rose and called out, 'Over here.' Scott wore a brown suit with a double breasted waistcoat, light blue shirt and a fawn wool tie. He had thin brown hair carefully arranged on a white scalp. As he came nearer to the seat his grim expression lightened a little, but he fitfully clenched his fists as if still carrying on an interior monologue.

Scott slumped down on the seat,

expelling air. He was obviously tense and sweating slightly. 'Sorry!' he said. 'Sorry about all this, but I know you're Charlie's oldest friend. I couldn't think of anyone else to talk to...' With his right hand he made an odd gesture towards the church as if it was in some way to blame for the situation that was worrying him. 'When I talked to Mrs Saunders this morning I didn't know what to say. She's obviously frantic and if I told her the truth it would have worried her more. So where does that leave me?' As Scott asked the question he swivelled round to face Quinn; his thick glasses magnified his grey eyes and seemed to lift them out of his face.

'You're worried because Charlie's gone off without saying anything?'

'That's part of it. Look, I've worked for the boss for twenty years so I know his ways. Yes, he's very impetuous and liable to dash off somewhere at the drop of a hat. He's in Cambridge and he hears of a good sale in Fort William, so he thinks nothing of driving all night to get there first thing. But never, no, not once, has he gone off without phoning to put us in the picture about outstanding business, appointments, that kind of thing. Well now he's been gone since last Friday and not a solitary word. And there's an important sale today, at Phillips. I know he was very keen on some of those items and had bids for clients, but I can't even find his marked catalogue—so there's nothing I can do about that. It's mighty strange—very worrying in fact.'

'Perhaps he went abroad?'

'Oh, I've thought of that. But the same rule applies. You know he would go to Paris like other people pop down to Brighton, but he always phoned.'

'And there's something else worrying you?'

'Too right there is!' Scott paused and surveyed the area in case anyone might be in earshot. He gestured at the church again. 'You know they've got some fine Gibbons things in there?'

'Gibbons?'

'Grinling Gibbons—1648 to 1721—master wood-carver. A suberb craftsman! Wonderful pieces!' Momentarily Scott's eyes gleamed and Quinn could see why he was a good salesman. 'Well, we had a piece by Gibbons once, a reredos.

The governor kept it hidden away in his small office upstairs. Then suddenly it had gone. I suspect that it was sold for cash. Afterwards I heard a rumour that it was decidedly iffy, a story that it had been stolen from some church in the Midlands...'

'But this was some time ago?'

'Yes it was. No, the point is that recently Charlie's been keeping some other things up in that office—they're still there in fact. You see, at the beginning of the year he went to inspect items in a French chateau—I can't remember where exactly. He enthused about them but said he thought it would be difficult to get an export licence, that they were of historical significance and therefore he didn't think the Froggies would let them go...' Scott paused again and sniffed significantly. 'Well, I'll swear that some of them are upstairs in Neal Street now. Under lock and key of course. But I have keys for every room and I had to search about while looking for that Phillips catalogue.'

'You think Charlie may have smuggled the French pieces?'

Scott nodded sagaciously. 'If not then

why all the secrecy? With things as good as that he's usually keen to show them to me and Mary Thompson. Sidney's not all that interested but Charlie knows we both take an interest in anything he's bought. He's got a fantastic flair for the business, finds things everywhere. And you know he likes to boast a bit. These French things must have been brought into the shop when no-one was about. There's a reason.'

Quinn said, 'I don't know if Mrs Saunders told you, Fred, but I'm trying to find out what's happened to Charlie. Now I've got what I think is a good lead and it seems to tie up with what you've told me. So I shall be looking into it tomorrow. If I'm lucky then I'll phone you Saturday. If not, then I shall ask Lilian Saunders to come to Neal Street on Monday and we shall all have to have another talk. About the shop, you're not short of cash to pay the wages?'

'No problem there. I can sign cheques. The business will tick on for a while...'

'Well, that's all right then. So let me worry about Charlie. Believe me, I shall do all I can.'

CHAPTER 21

As Quinn drove along a narrow road from which he had intermittent glimpses of the River Orwell the tune of 'Yesterday' was going round and round in his brain. The song had been a favourite of Madeleine's and he associated it with the early, happy years of their marriage. Yes, he acknowledged to himself, I do want yesterday back again, specifically that period when Dolly and Liz were young and completely adorable; then he realised that his feeling for his daughters was just part of the universal wish to hang on to what had gone. It was a futile desire and he dismissed the thought when he stopped his Mercedes in a village called Freston and consulted his Ordnance Survey map of 'Ipswich & The Naze areas'. Freston was only a mile or so from Woolverstone, where he would have to turn left for Pin Mill which was situated right on the river. From the map he could see that Pin Mill seemed to be well placed for smuggling as there were only two bends in the river beyond it before the open sea was reached. As he folded up the map Quinn was pondering on whether Charlie might be capable of embarking on something like smuggling antiques into the country. Charlie's morality was flexible: he was strongly opposed to all crimes of violence but tolerant of financial misdemeanours, and on tax matters he always argued, ''Course we self-employed geezers have got to help ourselves a bit—we're on our own aren't we?' Quinn knew for a fact that Charlie had occasionally broken the British export regulation on antiques, so it seemed quite possible that he would do the same in France.

Quinn was enjoying the drive in an area he had never seen before. Going down the lane from Woolverstone to Pin Mill the brightening sky and the uncluttered horizon gave him the feeling of approaching the sea. This impression grew stronger as he spied the pub right at the river's edge: 'The Butt & Oyster' had an idyllic setting for it appeared like part of a small harbour. There was a great deal of activity round about to do with boats, and a group of people sitting

191

outside the pub were visibly enjoying the active river scene. The Orwell was wide at Pin Mill and accommodated some large sailing barges as well as numerous yachts and motor cruisers. Quinn parked his car outside a house named 'Seagulls', thought for a moment then retrieved Charlie's diary from the front seat of the car before locking the doors.

He entered a long bar and luncheon area in the pub which had large picture windows looking out on the river. He asked a jovial, bald man behind the bar who was pulling a pint of beer, 'Can you tell me where I might find a Mr Shafto—William Shafto?'

The bald man grinned widely while still concentrating on the job in hand. 'No problem there Guv.' He checked that the tankard was full and then called out, 'Billy! Gent here enquiring for you.'

The barman's shout was directed at a man in his early thirties with short black hair and unusually heavy black eyebrows. He had a humourous, slightly twisted mouth and washy blue eyes; he looked very tanned and fit. Shafto was sitting at a small table, holding a half-empty tankard and talking to a woman with white hair like cake icing. When the barman called his name again Shafto stood up, saying 'All right! Okay!' He wore blue jeans, a navy crew-necked sweater and white tennis shoes; in his left hand he held steel aviator sunglasses. His lop-sided smile vanished as he took in Quinn's appearance and he looked serious, even perturbed.

Shafto approached the bar saying, 'You want me?' He looked suspicious.

'Yes, I'm Jack Quinn—a friend of Charlie Saunders. I wanted to talk to you about him.'

'I'm not talking in here. No sir! No way!'

'Shall we go outside?'

Shafto walked ahead, not saying anything until they were out of earshot of the pub customers seated outside. He walked along a path by the river that led upstream, past a sign which stated in four different languages: 'NO ANIMALS FROM ABROAD MAY BE LANDED'. Then he turned on his heel. 'How well do you know Charlie?'

'He's my best friend. I've known him since I was in short trousers. Are you checking up on me?'

'Just tell me something about him.'

193

'He's sixty-eight. Lost most of his hair on top. Brown eyes. Walks with a limp because he trod on a boobytrap in Normandy soon after D-day. He's married but hasn't got any children. Lives in Golders Green and has an antiques shop in Neal Street. Likes to talk, often tells Jewish jokes, has lots of Jewish friends. He's an expert on clocks. Five foot eight. Usually wears navy-blue suits...'

'Enough, enough! Okay, so you're a friend of Charlie's. What do you want to talk about?'

'Charlie's missing—he hasn't been seen since last Friday evening.'

'Are you serious?'

'One hundred per cent. Lilian—his wife—is very worried indeed.'

'Jesus!'

'What can you tell me?'

'Nothing here. We need somewhere completely private.' Shafto consulted a steel watch on his hairy thick wrist. 'Let's go to my boat. I need to think. What's that book you're holding?'

'Charlie's diary. He mentions you in it, and this place, and your boat "Why Not?".'

'Oh me oh my! I can't believe it! He

wrote all that down?'

'He did. I can show you.'

'Later.'

Shafto took a pathway between two houses, quickening his pace. In a minute they were at the edge of the hamlet, near a path running past a copse signposted 'Bridleway'. Shafto turned to face Quinn. 'It's quite a walk to my boat. I'm rather tucked away. Tell me more about why you've known Charlie so long. You must be nearer my age than his.'

'My father knew him just after the war, when Charlie first started in the antiques business. Charlie was what's called a runner then—that's the name for someone who buys things in small shops and sells them again upmarket—just dealing with the trade. My father had a second-hand shop in Hammersmith and Charlie often used to call in. I grew up calling him Uncle Charlie.'

As they skirted a cornfield Quinn glimpsed the river again through a row of trees which looked as if they had curvature of the spine. It was an even wider stretch of the Orwell, quite deserted apart from gulls that wheeled above it. Shafto said, 'When we have our chat you'll understand why

I've been so cagey. It's all very difficult. Your news was a shock, and hearing about that diary...' Shafto smiled bleakly. 'Funny thing. You never know about people. I wouldn't have dreamt that Charlie would write down everything in a diary.'

'He didn't write much. Just your name and the boat—dates he came to Pin Mill—that kind of thing.'

'That's too much, believe me. Well, here we are. This stretch of the river is called Potter Point. Very quiet.'

They had come to a stretch of boggy ground. A track of wooden planks laid over it led to the spot where a motor-cruiser, painted sea-green, was moored. The name WHY NOT? was in dark green paint.

Shafto grinned. 'When I bought her she was called FAST LADY, but I thought that sounded like boasting so I re-named her. But I've done a lot of work on the engines so now she's faster than when she was new.'

Quinn said, 'I know nothing about boats—never been on one like this.'

'Come aboard. It's reasonably comfortable and as private as can be.' Shafto stepped nimbly on to the stern of the boat. 'A modest place but I call it home.'

All the paintwork gleamed as if it had been done recently. In the cabin the only things on view were copies of the *Motor Boat* and the *Daily Mail* on a small table. Quinn took a seat, feeling particularly large and bulky in the confined space.

Shafto opened a cupboard to which was pinned an amateurish water colour of a moonlit river scene. He took out two glasses and a bottle of Glenmorangie malt whisky. 'Have a drink—all right?'

'Yes—thanks—why not?'

Shafto poured two generous helpings of the whisky which happened to be one of Quinn's favourite tipples, then sat down, stretching out his legs, looking very serious and thoughtful. 'Now tell me just once more—I'm a slow reader—about Charlie. You say that no-one's seen him since last Friday. Is that very unusual? He told me that he was always travelling.'

'That's right, he scours the country for antiques—but he never goes off without phoning his wife—and the man who manages his shop. This time—nothing, not a word.'

'And just checking up on the diary led you to me?'

'Yes, but don't worry about the diary

being seen by other people. Charlie kept it to himself, he only referred to it once in all the time I've known him. He used it like other people use a calendar—just to remind himself of appointments, things like that. He made a note about seeing you last Friday night, here at 2 to 3 am.'

'Can I see that note?'

'Sure!'

A nervous tick moved in Shafto's face as he studied the relevant page. He said, 'Does this entry for the evening—"Sotheby's party—ask Jacko about the Pickering Place party"—refer to you?'

'It does.'

'And did you meet "the terrible duo"?'

'I think so. I know that sounds like nonsense, but I had too much to drink that evening and blotted out. I do remember a striking looking blonde girl and I think that...'

'You're right—probably. Tall and slim with large green eyes?'

'That's her.'

Shafto bit his lip. 'Look, I like Charlie. We get on fine and I regard him as a friend so I want to help if I can. What I'm going to tell you could get me in big trouble so it's for your ears only—you understand?'

'Right.'

'I met Charlie—through a mutual friend who shall be nameless—last Christmas. He told me he was buying some antiques in France but there was a problem about getting them over here—he thought the authorities might be difficult. I told him that if he could get them to a particular spot on the French coast I could probably do the trick, providing there was nothing too big—I'm not in the removal business. He made some joke about having to dump the wardrobe. The funny thing is that I was already doing similar jobs for the couple he calls "the terrible duo". They told me they went round Europe, visiting remote churches and monasteries, buying up relics, icons. If you met them you could see how they might pull it off. A remarkable pair—like twins to look at. Tom and Tommy they called themselves—and they threw in the surname Smith, but I didn't put too much weight on it...'

'I think Tommy's real name is Tamsin Guild.'

'You *may* be right. I saw that name on an envelope once, when I contacted her through an accommodation address in New Cavendish Street. But I don't think

Tom's name is Guild. Charlie seemed to know what it was, I don't know how... He's rather fascinated by the pair of them.'

'Perhaps that's why he wanted me to meet them at the party.'

'You think so?'

'Oh yes, it was the kind of thing Charlie did with me, said it was "furthering my education".'

'I see. Well, now you'll understand why this is something I'm not going to admit outside this boat. I arranged a delivery for them last Friday night. They turned up here together okay but then things went wrong. Unloading the stuff wasn't easy in the dark and I didn't want any lights drawing attention to us. One of Tom's packages broke open...' Shafto grimaced and made a despairing gesture. 'Out of it fell a plastic packet of white powder. Charlie pounced on it in a flash, calling out, "What's this—drugs?"'

'Blimey!'

'You're shocked?'

'Yes, but not half as much as Charlie would be—his nephew died of an over-dose.'

'Talk about drama and farce! There we were, all involved in smuggling and liable for a stretch inside, and Charlie is shouting out that he won't have anything to do with drugs. I had to tell him to belt up.'

'What did the couple say?'

'Tommy said nothing. She always lets Tom do the talking—it's as if he's got her hypnotised. Tom made a joke—he's always joking in a cynical way—about it only being pleasure powder. Pleasure for the people he said.'

'I can just see Charlie going over the top. He's got a short fuse.'

'He exploded all right. But I managed to quieten them down. Frankly I wanted to wave goodbye to the lot of them. I'd already decided to have nothing more to do with "the special import business" as Charlie calls it.'

'They went off together?'

'They did. In Charlie's BMW. I saw the lights disappear at the end of the lane.'

'I shall have to find Tom.'

'That won't be easy. They're a slippery pair. When I contacted them first it was through this accommodation address. They were then staying at a small hotel in York Street, but Tommy told me they always used a different hotel.'

'I'll find him.'

'Well, good luck! Getting him to talk straight won't be easy.'

'I'll make him talk straight.' Normally Quinn didn't like making threats but he felt that this was a time for breaking rules.

CHAPTER 22

Tom parked his hired Ford Sierra near a signpost that was marked 'Bridleway', turned off the car's lights and sat back, relaxed, going over his immediate plans: he could foresee a tricky half hour since he did not under-estimate his opponent; Bill Shafto's behaviour was not easy to predict. It was 10 pm and the moon was temporarily hidden by cloud so it was quite dark. Tom was a little disguised in that his blond hair was concealed beneath a dark grey cap, and he wore an old navy-blue mac which was usually kept in his rented Thames-side house. He turned round to look at the scattered lights of houses in Pin Mill. Tom imagined all the inhabitants of the houses seated before television sets, doing their living by proxy, something he never did.

With a lop-sided smile, mimicking that of Bill Shafto, Tom got out of the Sierra and extracted his invaluable briefcase, then removed a large can of petrol from the boot and locked the car. A cold wind was blowing strongly from the east, stirring the trees and making a suitably mournful sound. Tom began to limp down the lane, carrying his briefcase and the can of petrol. There was nothing wrong with his legs but he felt that a limp went with the sinister 'Mr Tod' persona. In 'Mr Tod's' voice he said, 'Nothing personal, Bill, but you've outlived your usefulness, old chum, and you could be a problem.'

Compelled by some hereditary flaw and the bizarre circumstances of his childhood Tom was in a sense the captive of his depraved imagination, serving out a sentence of proving life to be an essentially meaningless affair. He stared up at the night sky in which the moon appeared to be playing a game of hide-and-seek with a succession of fast-moving clouds blown from the east. When the moon appeared completely unobscured a horse whinnied nearby and the sound sent a rare tremor of fear through Tom's limbs. He put down his briefcase and extracted a Roman coin, which he looked on as his lucky piece: it was his sole inheritance from his long dead father and it had come to him purely by chance. 'Heads I win' he said in 'Mr Tod's' voice. He tossed the silver coin and caught it in his palm with the noble profile upwards. 'Double or quits.' The process was repeated with another satisfactory result. In his normal voice he said his personal abracadabra: 'Nothing matters', picked up his case and walked on quickly.

When Tom reached the boggy strip of land that borders the River Orwell at Potter Point he was glad that the moon was again hidden so that he could approach Shafto's boat in darkness. He took off his cap and mac, smoothing back his long blond hair and straightening his tie so that he would appear his usual immaculate self. He left the can of petrol by his mac on the path of wooden planks but carried the briefcase with him to the boat. Tom had told Tommy, his only confidante, that he lived by the three i's—intuition, instinct and impulse. He felt that all three were compelling him to this confrontation with Shafto.

There were biggish waves on the Orwell, created by an ever-freshening breeze, and the boat WHY NOT? was bobbing sharply up and down. Tom stepped on to its stern as quietly and gracefully as a cat. He looked down into the cabin where Shafto was reading a paperback and said 'Surprise' in a cheerful voice.

Shafto looked up and said 'Oh yes' tonelessly, his eyes suspicious.

'I thought I ought to pop in, see that everything was okay and pay you a cash bonus.' Saying this, Tom extracted a roll of ten pound notes from an inner pocket of his grey flannel jacket.

'Why's that?'

'I had this feeling, call it intuition if you like, that you might be fed-up with the special imports business, and want to pack it in.'

'And the cash is to keep me quiet?'

''Course not. We were in it together. Well, just look on it as severance pay.' Tom threw the roll of notes, circled by an elastic band, to Shafto who caught it negligently in his left hand as if he had all the time in the world. Tom silently noted this further demonstration of Shafto's ultra-quick reactions and dexterity. He sat down by the entrance to the cabin and placed his open briefcase on the floor between his legs. He sighed and said, *Il mondo cane,* ain't that the truth.'

For a few moments Shafto said nothing and his silence seemed hostile. Then he put the roll of notes on the small table before him along with the paperback book. He said, 'Charlie Saunders seems to have disappeared. He hasn't been seen since he drove off with you last Friday night.'

Tom's expression of cat-like calm changed into a faint smile. 'I haven't seen Charlie since that night. We said our goodbyes in the Pier Road, North Woolwich. I wished him good luck.' Every word that Tom said was true so it was easy for him to be convincing.

'I had a chap come to see me here, Jack Quinn, a friend of Charlie's. He was very puzzled that Charlie should have gone off somewhere without even telling his wife. Quinn wanted to see you to ask you about it, but I couldn't provide him with your address.'

'No problem there, old chum. We are staying, for this trip only, at Duke's Head

Hotel, George Street.' Lies always tripped off Tom's tongue because they had become second nature to him, but again he told Shafto the truth, knowing it would do him no good.

Shafto visibly relaxed, his hunched shoulders dropped and his crooked grin appeared. 'That's good. Frankly that was a little mystery, about Charlie, that had me a good deal worried. I thought you were still quarrelling when you drove off.'

'I quietened him down, he became more reasonable.'

'No idea where he may have gone to?'

For the first time it became essential for Tom to lie. 'No idea at all.' He said it quickly, with a very clear mental picture of Charlie's last resting place, entombed with his smuggled antiques and his BMW in the Woolwich reach section of the Thames.

'Right, well, look.' Shafto produced his familiar lopsided smile. 'Look, here—I don't want this cash. It's true I've finished with the special imports lark but you don't owe me a thing. We're all square.' He pushed the roll of notes to the edge of the table and Tom leant forward to pocket them, saying, 'Okay—so we'll scrub that. Any chance of a farewell drink?'

Shafto scratched his chest and stretched his legs. 'Of course. Why not?'

When Shafto moved across to the cupboard where he kept a bottle of whisky Tom was tense, knowing that the next few seconds would be critical. While still seated Tom was mentally up on his toes, like a cat waiting to pounce. His face was calm but his sea-green eyes had the glitter of excitement.

Shafto whistled a few sharp notes so they sounded like the call sign to a message in Morse code, and straightened a painting that hung on the cupboard door. He stepped back a pace to see if it was straight and at that moment Tom seized his black cosh and struck Shafto a vicious blow on the back of his head. Shafto fell forward and down in a heap, dragging the painting with him.

Tom at once took a hypodermic syringe from his briefcase and pushed up a sleeve of Shafto's heavy white pullover to disclose an arm packed with muscle. With a dexterity born of practice he massaged up a vein and injected a lethal dose of heroin. 'Just pleasure powder, old chum.' He replaced the syringe in his case and said, 'The thing about H—it makes it unnecessary to worry about the things you have been worrying about.'

Shafto lay on his side, his bare right arm stretched out, his face devoid of expression, his baby-blue eyes open but glazed.

When Tom stepped off the boat luck was on his side, as it often was, and the moon was completely hidden by cloud. Nevertheless he had a careful look round as it was vital that his next act should not be seen. He stood still listening intently in case there was a boat moving in the direction of Potter Point. Then he placed his briefcase on the wooden planks and disguised himself with the mac and cap. He carried the can of petrol to the boat with the plan of leaving a sizeable amount splashed about the cabin and just a trail of it from the cabin to the stern. When that job was completed he threw the can into the cabin. He laid a fuse from the stern to the pathway, looked round once more, then lit the fuse.

Tom thought that he had judged his departure carefully but the boat started to burn with flames leaping into the sky before he had reached the shelter of the trees, and it was accompanied by two small explosions that he had not expected. By the time he was walking in the shadow of the trees the whole boat was enveloped in flame. The force of a third explosion also surprised him—it was like a massive firework display accompanied by a shattering bang which he knew was liable to wake all the inhabitants of Pin Mill. Bits of the boat fell from the sky. For a few minutes the hulk of the boat burnt intensely, then it suddenly vanished beneath the surface of the river. Tom said woodenly, 'Death clears the board.'

CHAPTER 23

Saturday, October 3rd, 1987

The day started for Jack Quinn with the rat-tat of the postman at his door. The sound woke him from a nightmare in which fact was mixed with gibberish and contained a jolting vision of Charlie Saunders disappearing into a tunnel. Quinn was glad to wake up and as it was unusual for him to receive mail at his Bourdon Street address he hurried downstairs in his pyjamas, hoping it would not be a buff envelope containing a bill. Instead there was a narrow envelope of blue laid paper lying face down on the mat. It was an elegant envelope and he turned it over without a clue as to his correspondent, but that became clear the moment he saw his address written in jet black ink because he knew that large pointed writing was Anna's. Inside the envelope there was a matching coloured card:

Darling MacHeath
'How like a moth, the simple maid
Still plays about the flame'
    THE BEGGAR'S OPERA, 1, iv
'If with me you'll fondly stray,
Over the hills and far away.'
    THE BEGGAR'S OPERA, 1, xiii
    Love from Anna

Perhaps it was the fates, the Parcae, the three goddesses supposed to preside over the course of human existence, who planned two phone calls for Quinn which were to shape an eventful day. The first came while he was standing in his kitchen, staring at the blue card which he had propped up against an empty tea cup. He glanced at his watch to see that it was only 7.35 am and became hopeful that such an early call would be from Charlie, setting fears at rest. He snatched up the phone but instead of Charlie's voice he heard his daughter Dolly, sounding very bubbly and excited. She explained that she would not be calling in to see him, as was usual on Saturday mornings: 'Sorry, Dad, but we're off to Cambridge in a few minutes. For the weekend! Staying in a hotel tonight!' Then Liz took over to add: 'Sorry, Daddy, but we'll make it without fail next Saturday. Mum says we must rush now—have to catch a train at Liverpool Street!' Quinn was disappointed that he would not be seeing his girls but was amused by their excitement over the trip. They both loved travelling and doing anything new, and their naive enthusiasm momentarily swept him back to a long-ago epoch when everything had been fresh and potentially exciting.

As he went into the bathroom to shave and shower Quinn was thinking about the girls' destination. Cambridge meant that Madeleine was going to see a university don called Geoffrey Brown, a new friend, of whose existence he had only heard by occasional comments from his daughters.

If Madeleine was prepared to make an expedition involving the girls in order to see Brown that must mean she was seriously interested in the man—a development that might have all kinds of implications. Quinn was not jealous but he feared any changes that might affect his relationship with his daughters.

If the first phone call slightly perturbed Quinn it had nothing like the effect of the second which came just as he had covered his face with shaving cream and made one stroke with the razor. It was June Whitall, also sounding rather bubbly: 'A Mr Toby Walters phoned yesterday afternoon. He said that General Erskine had asked him to contact you about the Gerald Despain German diary. Mr Walters is going away this morning for a long weekend in the country but he can see you between 9 and 10 am if that suits you. So I said he could expect you on the dot of nine. Did I do right?'

'Absolutely, Kiddo. You could not have done righter. I very much want to see Mr Walters and it may mean a good stroke of biz. Where does he live?'

'He has a flat in Pickering Place. Said you have to go through a narrow passageway to it, in St James's Street, just by the side of the wine merchants, Berry Bros, no 3. Is that okay?'

It was Jack Quinn's turn to feel excited and mystified but he said, 'Fine. Thanks June. See you Monday morning.'

Quinn went back to the bathroom and finished shaving while his mind was in a whirl concerning all the possibilities of June's revelation. It was clear that the mysterious Friday night party must have taken place in Toby Walters' flat so that he had been entertained, albeit while he was in an alcoholic haze, by Gerald Despain's nephew. And by simply visiting the flat in Pickering Place he would probably be able to learn something about 'the terrible duo' as well as discover whether the Despain German diary might be sold. Any question Quinn asked himself simply raised further questions, and vague memories only added to the confusion so that in the end he had to make a great effort to keep his mind blank while he finished shaving, ate his muesli breakfast and did the usual chores he performed every morning.

★ ★ ★ ★

Quinn arrived at the Pall Mall end of St James's Street at ten minutes to nine so he had to kill time by looking in shop windows. Lobb, the prestigious bootmakers, and Lock, the famous hatters, both had unique displays but Quinn was mentally drumming his fingers with impatience so that their goods hardly registered as he waited until he could pass through the narrow passageway by the side of the wine merchants.

He did so just as a nearby clock struck the hour, noting that Pickering Place was identified by the usual London nameplate and puzzled therefore that it should not be listed in the London street directory. He stood still for a moment in the delightful little courtyard, trying to force a memory of having been there the previous Friday, but his capricious brain would not collaborate. As he walked up some stairs he heard Charles Trenet singing *La Mer*, an old record he knew well as he had a copy that had belonged to his mother. A door was open and he heard a man's voice saying, 'Mr Quinn? Do come in. I spied you from the window. The General was right. You are indeed punctual.'

Quinn walked through a hallway with

French-grey walls which were decorated with two Andrew Wyeth paintings, and into a large room with a high ceiling. A tall man smiled and said, 'Morning, Mr Quinn. I say, you certainly made a good impression on General Erskine. He said I ought to meet you because of your interest in my notorious uncle, but he added that you were punctual, efficient and discreet.'

'Well, I enjoyed meeting the General. I had a very nice day at Nantyffin.'

'Funny thing is, if you'd taken his fancy in 1944 you'd probably have ended up dead. He was like General Patton, always wanting to attack... Do take a pew.'

A huge Chinese vase stood in a nearby corner, and a large sofa and two armchairs with cream linen loose covers were grouped round a television set at the far end. Quinn tried to imagine the room full of people as it had been during the Friday night party, but it did not strike a responsive chord.

Toby Walters was in his early forties. He wore a brown check sports coat, a dark brown roll-neck pullover and baggy corduroy trousers. He had a prognathous chin and large white teeth like his uncle but there was a vital difference in expression: whereas Gerald Despain stared boldly out of photographs, seeming to say 'to hell with you', Toby Walters had a mild, friendly look. His face was asymmetrical—one side was austere with a drooping eyelid; the other was quizzical with a light, beaming blue iris.

Quinn sat down and said, 'I think I should tell you that I've been here before. At your party last Friday. A friend called Charlie Saunders invited me to come when I was in an alcoholic haze. Then I must have had quite a lot of your good champagne and passed out in the street. When I woke up I was in St Mary's Hospital. So I should apologize...'

'Oh no need, old chap. I invited about fifty bods and I should think seventy or eighty turned up here. Friends brought friends, that sort of thing. They know I don't mind. I never worry, it's a good way of meeting new people.'

'It's not the sort of thing I usually do but I'd been to a party at Sotheby's and the drink I took on board there must have clashed with some tablets I was taking. So I would have to plead guilty but hazy.'

'I don't remember meeting you but I was in rather a whirl myself, and there was a great crush. "Hardly standing room only" as some joker said. You don't remember much about the do I take it?'

'Very little. Just chatting to an attractive blonde girl who I'm told is called Tamsin Guild.'

'I see. And did you meet her friend Tom?'

'Not that I remember.'

'Ah, well Tom is the reason why you're having a largely wasted trip this morning. You see, I can't sell you the German diary or even show it to you because I gave it to Tom who is Gerald Despain's son.'

'My God! So the son did survive?'

'Yes, survive is the right word for it. Tom spent three years in a state orphanage from 1945 until his aunt Gretl Schellenberg decided to adopt him. And my mother said that was like falling out of the frying-pan into the fire. You see, my Mama actually met Gretl, a fanatical Nazi like her sister, and obsessed with discipline. Apparently Gretl believed that the ghastly Adolph had been let down by the mass of the German people because they lacked discipline.'

'Does Tom look like his father?'

'Very much so—the spitting image in

218

fact. And he usually wears a grey flannel suit with white shirt and black tie like Gerald during his Nazi period.'

'What's your cousin like?'

Walters sniffed and gave the matter thought. 'Ah now, that's a difficult question. My mother says that Tom is impossible to know, and I think that's fair. He's like a chameleon, puts on a different act to suit each situation. He's very intelligent, fluent in four languages, but he's cynical, doesn't seem to believe in anything. Obsessed with gambling—he literally would be willing to gamble on raindrops running down a window. I'm told he owes big gambling debts in London at the moment. But any amount of cash won't persuade him to part with Gerald's Nazi diary.'

'Nevertheless I very much want to meet him.'

'Anything to do with money?'

'No, money doesn't come into it. It's an important matter concerning a friend of mine.'

'I see. Well it would have to be an extremely important matter for you to see him just at present. I happen to know that he and Tamsin are going abroad today.'

Walters glanced at his watch. 'In fact they should be airborne at this moment.'

'Do you know where?'

'I do. They're going to the only place they regard as home—Paxos, a very small Greek island to the south of Corfu. They own a tiny cottage there, situated at the bottom of a cliff. I can show you a postcard if you like.'

'Please.'

'Right.' Walters stood up. 'If you're really serious, if you do think of going all that way, you'd have to stay in a little place called Loggos. Two years ago Tamsin suggested that I should have a holiday there but said I would have to stay in Loggos since they have only one bedroom. Apparently Loggos is just a cluster of houses and tavernas round a harbour. Hold on a moment.'

When Walters returned his said in a stagey voice, 'The cliffs of Eremitis on the island of Paxos.' He held up a picture postcard and said, 'Hard to imagine anywhere more isolated than their "retreat". Still they seem to like it. It seems you have to scramble down the cliff to it. Their water comes from a spring.'

The postcard showed a view of towering cliffs beyond a row of cypress trees. Walters said, 'Read what it says, nothing private. Typical Tamsin stuff.'

Walter's Pickering Place address was written in a small stylish script, as legible and attractive as Oscar Wilde's. The message was brief:

Dear Toby,
Heaven again! "And in that heaven of all their wish"—R Brooke. Or as near to Heaven as we ever hope to be. So, see what you miss in not coming here!
Love, Tamsin

Walters made an inconclusive gesture, saying, 'By the way, you can't fly direct to Paxos. You have to take a ferry boat from Corfu, a three hour trip I think. So it would be quite an expedition.'

Quinn handed back the card. 'Thanks. That's very helpful.'

Walters shook his head unbelievingly. 'So shall you really be sailing across the Ionian Sea?'

'Yes, it's something I've promised to do.'

CHAPTER 24

Sunday, October 4th, 1987

Flying at 30,000 feet, somewhere over France and bound for Corfu, Jack Quinn ordered a small bottle of red Rioja, sat back and relaxed for the first time in what had been a strange sort of day. At Gatwick airport, waiting for a much delayed flight, he had felt decidedly odd among the crowds of happy holidaymakers while he was on what might well prove to be a wild goose chase. The people at the airport had been largely middle-aged couples or families with children who were not of school age, but there was one girl who looked about as old as Dolly, running about and talking excitedly to her parents, and that had reminded him with a pang of being at Gatwick the previous year, setting off for a family holiday in Positano. At that moment his quest to find Tom Despain had seemed absurd: he had only Toby Walters' word that 'the terrible duo' had gone to Paxos, so going there himself was certainly like backing a longshot, but he had seen no alternative. He was determined to find out what had happened to Charlie, and the finger of suspicion pointed at Tom Despain. Going to the police was not a possibility any longer since that might lead to prison sentences for all who had been involved in the smuggling at Pin Mill. While Quinn had no objection to the cynical Despain serving a stretch inside he could not risk involving Charlie, Bill Shafto and Tamsin Guild.

Quinn had an aisle seat so that he did not feel cramped. Next to him there was a pleasant Welsh couple in their fifties who had smiled and said 'Good morning', ironically accentuating the word 'morning' because they were all setting off some three hours late on their Air Europe flight. A blue canvas bag at Quinn's feet contained two short-sleeved shirts, pants and socks, a toilet bag and a paperback copy of *Dombey and Son*. He felt that no-one on the plane would be travelling so light and have so few plans. His one obsessive thought was to find Tom Despain.

There was laughter coming from behind

him and Quinn turned round to hear a group querying whether lunch or tea would be served on the delayed flight. Moments later they heard the pilot's voice apologising for the late start, announcing that a hot meal would be served during the flight, and that the estimated Greek time of their arrival in Corfu was 6 pm. The announcement caused a ripple of laughter and chatter. Quinn grinned and relaxed some more. These were the sort of people he understood best and felt at home with, couples who had worked hard for their package holidays and were going to enjoy them despite delays and disappointments.

'Your drinks, sir.' The smiling hostess jerked Quinn out of his introspection. The middle-aged couple had both ordered orange juice. When their drinks had been placed on folding trays the slightly built man said in a lilting voice, 'We couldn't help noticing the Paxos label on your bag. That's our destination too. Do you know the island well?'

'No, I've never been there. I went to Corfu years ago, but this is my first time for Paxos.'

'You're in for a treat then! We went there for the first time on a day trip from

Corfu in 1980, and we've been back every year. Nowhere like it, well, that's what we think—if you want a peaceful break. Oh, by the way, we're David and Gwen Williams.'

'Jack Quinn.'

'You'll find Paxos is nothing like Corfu. No discos or any sort of modern entertainment. It's very small, only six by two miles. And the whole island is covered with olive trees which were planted by the Venetians. Olive trees, small beaches and churches—that's Paxos. Over sixty chapels and churches, and only two of them are in ruins. Your label says Loggos. Are you renting an apartment there?'

'No, I've nothing booked. I decided to go on an impulse so I shall have to look for a place to stay.'

'Ask Nassos. He's the plump chap who runs the biggest taverna in Loggos, right on the front, with a green sun-blind. He'll fix you up with a room. Nassos knows everything there is to know about the island. And his taverna's the best place to eat in Loggos.'

'Have you ever been to the cliffs of Eremitis?'

'Once. It's a remote spot. You walk past

a handful of little houses at a place called Boikatika, and a tiny church, the Aghii Apostoloi. The best view of the cliffs is from the sea, but you can't row there yourself, it's too tricky.'

'Thanks. That's very helpful,' said Quinn as he jotted down the information.

Williams turned to talk to his wife and an image of Gerald Despain slotted itself into Quinn's mind. He thought that confronting Tom Despain would be much like having a showdown with his Nazi father, and quite relished the idea, but did not like the prospect of it taking place in the presence of Tamsin Guild. Quinn found it difficult to understand why Tamsin should go along with Despain's drug-smuggling activities, then remembered Bill Shafto saying of her, 'She always lets Tom do the talking—it's as if he's got her hypnotised.'

★ ★ ★ ★

Seated on the top deck of the ferry-boat 'Anna Maria', for a while Quinn had no desire to read. The boat's departure from Corfu had been delayed until 7 pm Greek time because of the late arrival of the Air Europe flight, so the three hour voyage over the Ionian Sea was taking place as the sun went down behind the seemingly endless line of hotel blocks and other developments along the coast of Corfu. To the east was the distant, mountainous coastline of Albania. The sky was continually changing colour and the effect of steaming off in the sunset was so peaceful that it dispelled Quinn's thoughts of what lay before him.

'Thought you might like this.' David Williams stood by his side, holding out a brightly coloured map of Paxos. 'We have two it seems. And this one we bought in Loggos so there's a picture of the little harbour there on the back cover. You'll need a map if you really want to find the cliffs of Eremitis. There are very few signposts on the island.'

'Great. Many thanks. Can I pay you for it?'

Williams brushed the suggestion aside. 'Forget it. You'll get off the boat before we do because Loggos is the first stop and we go on to Gaios, more to the south of the island. If you run short of drachmas there's an exchange in Loggos and you can buy most things there. Perhaps we'll see you one evening chez Nassos?'

227

'Yes, perhaps. Thanks again for your help.'

The coastline of Corfu had been left behind and the sun was descending into the open sea, appearing to send out a sequined path. Overhead the sky was a pale duck-egg blue imperceptibly shading into an apricot layer by the sun. Quinn picked up his paperback Dickens and read until the sun vanished. The 'Anna Maria' glided over a still sea. He could tell the boat must be nearing its destination when people crowded to the front where their luggage was stored.

Williams appeared once more. 'Now don't forget, ask Nassos for a room. Or his wife if he's away. Good luck!'

'Thanks. Happy holiday!'

A wooded coastline, devoid of lights and buildings, came into view. People waiting to disembark were chattering excitedly and forming into a queue. As he took his place Quinn had an image of Charlie slot into his mind, Charlie looking doubtful and uncertain what to do. He had a strong presentiment that Charlie was dead. When Lilian had expressed that fear he had dismissed it, saying that she could not *know*, but now he had the same conviction.

It was as if it had been said in his mind, expressed in a dull, matter-of-fact voice. Quinn sighed deeply as the 'Anna Maria' turned into a small bay and manoeuvred towards a jetty on the left-hand side.

People disembarking strode off purposefully with their luggage. Quinn stood still, looking round at Loggos. There were three small white-washed buildings on the jetty and another dozen or so grouped round the harbour. Land rose steeply behind the buildings, and the wooded hilly view outlined against a deep purple sky and a huge moon added to the sensation of peace. The warm night air was scented with herbs. He could see what appeared to be three tavernas with people at tables grouped outside. He walked over to the biggest one which was centrally placed. There was a good smell of grilled meat and garlic. He found an empty table and within moments was handed a simple menu by a young girl with curly dark brown hair. She guessed his nationality and said 'Good evening,' smiling.

'Hallo. Is this Nassos' place?'

'Oh yes. He is my father.'

'Good. I want to ask him something.'

'Little later. He is busy in the kitchen.'

Quinn ordered a bottle of retsina, chicken, chips and a salad. Once the retsina appeared, with some bread and olives, he determined to enjoy the meal and try to forget his depressing thoughts. Voices round him were mainly British but here was a large table of young Germans. Talk between the tables indicated that most people knew each other. Quinn thought how delightful it would be to be on holiday in Loggos with Anna Campaspe, with no problems and nothing to think of but where to swim and walk the following day.

The simple meal was excellent. When he had finished it a jovial-looking man with grey curly hair came to his table, saying 'I am Nassos. My daughter... Can I help you?'

'I hope so. I need a room for the night.'

Nassos raised his large right hand and grinned. He had the look of a man who relished life. 'That is easy. A clean, cheap room? Two thousand drachmas?'

'Fine. Does it have a bath or shower?'

'Yes. You like to go there now? Six-fifty drachmas for the meal...'

Quinn gave him three thousand drachmas,

indicating that he did not want any change.

Nassos grinned again and pointed to one of the buildings on the jetty. 'Over there. You have coffee here in the morning. I show you.'

As they walked over to the jetty, Nassos asked 'How long? One night?'

'I don't know at the moment,' Quinn said, facing the fact that he might have come to this remote island to achieve nothing. Suddenly he felt weary and the prospect of a shower and bed seemed the most desirable thing in the world. They walked past a very small bar where locals were watching television and went round to the back of the first building. Outside stone steps led up to the second floor. Nassos opened the door and switched on a light to disclose a room as bare of decoration as a monk's cell with one religious print on a white-washed wall. The window faced out over the harbour to the northern headland of the bay. There was a single divan, and one chair near to a hand-basin. A white rubber curtain half hid a shower and lavatory.

'Okay?' queried Nassos. 'Is there soap?'

'Yes, fine.' Quinn pointed to the basin where there was soap and a small towel.

'Everything I need.'

'Goodnight then. We see you in the morning.'

Quinn started to undress the moment the door closed. He opened the window wide and breathed in the faintly salty night air. There was no wardrobe but he hung his jacket up on a wire hanger on the back of the door. His shirt, trousers, pants and socks went on the chair. The water in the shower was only tepid but that seemed just right and he stayed beneath it until it ran cold. He had forgotten to bring pyjamas so he got into the deliciously cool sheets naked. He made an effort to read the Penguin Dickens but his mind would not take in the printed words because it was full of thoughts of Charlie, Lilian, Bill Shafto, the enigmatic Tamsin and Tom Despain, so he dropped the book and stared up at the moonlit sky. When he switched off the feeble electric bulb a firefly kept him company until he fell into a deep, dreamless sleep.

CHAPTER 25

The cliffs of Eremitis on the island of Paxos.

Sweating freely and squinting in the extraordinarily bright light, Quinn paused on the dusty road from Mastoratika to Magazia, then moved into the chequered shade of the olive trees which grew on both sides of the road. He had been woken early by cocks crowing at Loggos and that sound, together with the tinkling of goat-bells, had followed him all the way on his walk. He had been passed by only one vehicle in half an hour and that was a van full of live chickens going in the opposite direction. He had seen no-one else though once he heard the sound of voices from a remotely perched small house. Quinn was surprised by the heat in October and by the fact that the island seemed much larger than the Welshman on the plane had led him to believe. He imagined that this was due to Paxos being very hilly, so that any journey involved winding roads. Most of the walk from Loggos was uphill and the steepest stretches proved that he was not so fit as he had been a few years before. But, he thought grimly, years in the boxing ring had left him with enough skill to knock Tom Despain to the ground if that should prove necessary.

The cloudless sky was of an unusually vivid blue and some quality of the light made all the other colours intense: as if to confirm this a brilliant yellow and orange butterfly alighted near his feet and then danced along the road. As he looked round at the beautiful island Quinn thought again how much he would enjoy a holiday in such surroundings with Anna Campaspe. He remembered her langourous manner, her enigmatic smiles, the black ellipses drawn round her eyelids, and her long eyelashes fluttering against his cheek. He whistled the first part of the tune 'Let it be me' and sighed, thinking that his confrontation with Tom Despain might leave him never wishing to see Paxos again.

The road to Magazia was shadier than the one uphill from Loggos so he made better time and no longer felt that he was sweating. As he approached a little cluster of stone houses he saw a man leaning against a wall and cursed himself for having only a four-word Greek vocabulary. The man, a wide-hipped, sedentary looking character, holding some orange beads on a string, looked at him with interest. Quinn asked 'Boikatika?', gesturing vaguely to the western side of the island. The man grinned, nodded and gestured in a similar manner.

'Eremitis?'

'Eremitis.'

Quinn said thanks in English and quickened his pace. Within a matter of fifteen minutes, he estimated, he would know if he had wasted his time and money in coming to the island. How flat he would feel if the walk only led to a boarded-up cottage by the cliffs. Madeleine would say that it was typical of his ever impulsive approach to life.

The tarmac track to the west of the island led into a densely wooded area. The only signs of human activity were piles of neatly folded black nets used to catch the olives. He came upon a small green snake asleep on the track which showed how little it must be used. There was political graffiti in red paint on a derelict stone hut, including the initials KEA and XEK and a drawing of a hammer and sickle. When he came to the handful of tiny cottages which comprised Boikatika there was no-one to be seen though he could hear the gobbling of turkeys.

Beyond the village, on steeply rising ground, Quinn saw a small church of extreme simplicity, built with white distempered walls and a terracotta tiled roof. He walked up to it and tried the heavy wooden door, but it was locked. As he stood there wondering which way to go he remembered Dolly, as a four-year old, asking in a querulous voice, 'But who *is* God?' He thought: I want the life I had.

After a few minutes Quinn descended the slope and saw that a rough path through the undergrowth led off from the tarmac track, with signs of it having been used by some sort of vehicle. Following the path for a few yards took him away from the trees and into the open with a splendid view of the cliffs of Eremitis, much higher and more impressive than they had appeared in the postcard Tamsin Guild had sent to Toby Walters.

Away from the shade of the olive trees

the heat was terrific: the sun looked like a ball of fire against the vivid blue sky. The sea appeared to be largely cobalt blue with patches of turquoise and ultramarine. All he could hear was the faint sound of a cock crowing, and insects in the undergrowth. Empty cartridge-cases indicated that it was a place occasionally used for shooting, but this part of the island still seemed largely uninhabited. It was plain that Tamsin Guild's idea of heaven was somewhere remote from people. After a few more steps he saw a small black vehicle pushed off the path and walked along to inspect it—an old three-wheeler van with a carton of empty Retsina bottles and a large pair of black sandals in the back. A white signpost, roughly lettered DESPAIN in red paint, pointed towards the cliff's edge. Quinn was sweating again, so much so that a portion of his dark blue shirt was black and clinging to his ribs. His leather-soled shoes were a handicap in descending the cliff path and he imagined himself, hot, sweating and dusty, confronting Tamsin Guild who no doubt had the trick of remaining a Botticelli beauty, cool and self-possessed in any situation.

Quinn took a deep breath, thinking:

This is it. He remembered Mrs Vavasour quoting General Erskine saying 'We must all continue to go forward.' He started the downward journey badly by slipping on the first part and having to wildly grasp densely packed vegetation to keep upright, but as he descended further he evolved a technique of edging towards his goal. At first he had to concentrate on where he was putting his feet but soon reached a point where he could crane forward and see the Despain house, a small building of white stone built on a ledge so that its back wall appeared to touch the cliff. A stone balcony ran round the house and there were steps from it to a narrow beach of white sand. A rowing boat, painted Greek blue with the name CHANCE in white lettering, was pushed up on the beach.

A moment later Quinn saw Tamsin Guild, swimming nude in a stretch of turquoise coloured sea about twenty feet from the beach. She was doing the breast stroke, holding her head up to keep her blonde hair dry. Quinn paused, off balance and irresolute. What do I say? he thought. But a moment later he spotted another figure walking along the white sand; it was Tom Despain, looking immaculate but over-dressed for the beach, wearing a white suit with a black shirt. Despain's long blond hair was greased back at the sides, otherwise he looked very much like the photographs of his father.

Quinn's left foot slipped, disturbing some stones, and Despain looked up, appearing annoyed. 'Yes?' he said, 'What do you want here? This is a private beach.'

'My name is Quinn. I'm a friend of Charlie Saunders.'

'Ah yes, Mr Quinn. Bill Shafto said something about you.'

'I want to ask you some questions.'

Despain smiled and lifted his prognathous chin in an aggressive expression. 'And what if I don't want to answer them?'

'I'm not leaving here without some answers that make sense.' Quinn raised his big fists. 'If I have to, I'll flatten you.'

'Really?'

'Yes, and you know what? I think I shall enjoy it. I think you must be about as twisted as your mad old man.'

Despain smiled. 'Good, I'm glad you said that. Well, I can tell you that any questions concerning the late Mr Saunders should be addressed care of Old Father Thames.'

Quinn felt as though he had been hit on the head. Shock and rage left him speechless. He shook his left fist at Despain who smiled and said, 'So, goodbye Mr Quinn,' pulling out a small nickel-plated automatic from his jacket pocket. 'Now—a permanent arrangement.'

Three things happened at once: Tamsin screamed 'Don't! Don't!' from the sea, Despain glanced round at her, momentarily distracted, and Quinn leapt down at him. In mid-air Quinn heard the sound of a shot and felt as if he had been tapped on his upper right arm. He collided with Despain and they both fell to the ground. They got up simultaneouly and Despain swung his right fist round in a clumsy attempt at a punch. Quinn side-stepped this blow and grinned. Despain was strong and fit but did not seem to know how to fight with his hands. Quinn's years of boxing had left him with footwork and ring-craft which kept him immune from wild punches. A quick glance at his right arm confirmed that he had been shot but the wound was not painful and a left hand jab had always been his best weapon in a fight. It flicked out now in a quick succession of blows to Despain's eyes and mouth. Despain looked round, wildly searching for the automatic which had fallen on the beach, and Quinn connected with a solid punch to Despain's big jaw. The blow rocked him back on his heels and he blinked as if he could not see straight. Two more jabs opened up cuts on his face and a third one split his top lip.

Quinn heard quick footsteps behind him and then he felt puny blows on his back. Tamsin shouted out, 'Stop this! Please stop!' but Quinn was deaf to her pleas and continued to jab away at Despain's face. Then he landed another hard punch to the point of the chin which sent Despain to the ground. Once there he showed no sign of getting up and his eyes rolled back. Quinn picked up the Beretta and squatted on the beach, holding the automatic so that it was pointed at Despain's right knee.

For a few minutes Quinn said nothing but waited to get his breath back and to have Despain's attention. He saw Tamsin run up the steps which led to the small stone house. When Despain's eyes opened Quinn said, 'Now this is what we're going to do. We'll take your van into Gaios and find the police. You can accuse me of assault and I'll bring a charge of attempted murder, and I've got the bullet wound to convince them. I'm going to tell them that you are a drug smuggler and suggest they take a very careful look at your hut here. Somehow I'll convince them they should hold on to both of us until they contact the police in England. And when I get back there I shall tell the police that you've admitted killing Charlie, and the whole story of smuggling at Pin Mill. One way or the other I shan't rest until you are in the dock. You can rely on it.'

Despain lifted himself up on his elbows. He said nothing but spat fragments of a tooth and some bloody phlegm on Quinn's shirt.

CHAPTER 26

The trial of Thomas Walters Despain at the Central Criminal Court for the murder of Detective Inspector James Ross in a house in Pier Road, Woolwich, E16, began on Friday January 24, 1988. It was a very cold day with traces of frozen snow remaining on the streets, and a bitter east wind. No doubt the freezing weather kept the crowds away from the Old Bailey but nevertheless Jack Quinn had to take his place in a queue outside the building in order to enter No 1 court. He had never been to a trial before but was set on having the satisfaction of seeing Tom Despain in the dock.

Quinn's clothing summer and winter was usually the same, consisting of dark blue cotton shirt, grey tweed jacket and dark blue trousers, but on the day of the trial he had also donned an old navy-blue donkey jacket which Madeleine said was shabby. When he had been in the queue for a few minutes he heard his christian name being called out in a 'little girl' voice that was vaguely familiar. He turned round to see Mrs Rex Vavasour some distance back in the queue. She had left off her make-up and looked older and more vulnerable without it. She wore a long black coat and a hat which did not suit her. He walked back and then surprised himself by saying 'Hello Daphne' and taking her small, gloved hand. Mrs Vavasour gave him an intent look as if she had trouble in focusing her iodine-coloured eyes. She inclined her face while clinging to his hand and he kissed her cold cheek.

'What an extraordinary business!' she exclaimed. 'Gerald's son on trial for murdering a policeman! I can't believe it! That young reporter with the tabloid rag phoned me, said the rumour was that Tom may have killed other people too. A drug smuggler! Quite unbelievable!'

Quinn said quietly, 'I believe it. But it's a long story, too long to explain now. Perhaps I can call in at the Hall one day so we can have a talk?'

'Yes, please do. I meant to phone you anyway, Jack. Rex bought a lot of old books. Old maps too.' She gestured vaguely. 'That kind of thing. I don't want them...'

'Right, so I'll be in touch. Tell me, what does the General think about this trial?'

'He says Tom must be mad, blames it on "Bad blood", says there was a great-uncle, on the Walters side of the family, who was locked up as being insane... But did you know that Jumbo is in hospital?'

'No—and I saw him at the end of November.'

'He went in just before Christmas. He keeps things to himself.' Mrs Vavasour's sensitive mouth quivered and Quinn could see fear in her dark eyes. 'It's very serious.'

She lowered her voice. 'I think it's cancer.'

Quinn was silent for a moment, thinking about the General whom he had come to like as well as admire. He tried to imagine Erskine having to settle down to hospital discipline, and accommodate his large frame to a narrow bed.

He said, 'The General donated the money for the Despain papers to Cancer Research.'

'Ah, but that would be in memory of Louise, his wife. You see she died of cancer about five years ago.'

'Where is he?'

'The King Edward Hospital, in Beaumont Street.'

'I know it. I'll go and see him.'

'I'm sure he'd like that.'

'I must get back in the queue. So I'll phone you at the end of the month, then I'll tell you all I know about Tom Despain.'

'Goodbye then Jack.'

As Quinn took his place in the queue it began to move forward. He was comparing his life to Daphne's, imagining her mooning about in the big house which had been turned into a kind of shrine to Rex Vavasour, MP. Comparatively his own life seemed quite good. Madeleine showed no sign of leaving London to marry the Cambridge don—she had not mentioned the word divorce; his girls' routine of calling in to see him on Saturday mornings had expanded into their spending most of that day with him; he had spent Christmas Day at the Barton Street house on amicable terms with Madeleine; he had thrown away all the cartons in his mews house, and shelved his books and records so that it no longer looked 'a tip'. As he edged forward he thought: Yes, I've much to be thankful for. He was even becoming accustomed to a bachelor existence and gradually learning to cook.

Quinn heard a woman in a fur coat mention Despain's name and his thoughts again turned to vengeance and the irony of the situation. Despain had denied making the death taunt concerning Charlie and police divers had searched the Thames near Pier Road in Woolwich without finding the missing BMW, so that was a mystery which might never be solved. And while Despain was suspected of being involved in Bill Shafto's strange death, the police were doubtful that a murder case could be brought because of the lack of evidence. Chief Inspector Dando, at Scotland Yard, had explained all this succinctly to Quinn, but added in a quiet voice with a South London accent: 'Don't worry about Despain going free. We've got him. Oh yes! He made some mistakes.' Then he said, in the light unemphatic voice which somehow contrived to be threatening: 'Jimmy Ross was a very popular guy round here, he had a lot of friends. Despain trussed Jimmy up like a mummy and left him to choke in a cupboard.' Dando had paused and reflectively sucked a tooth before adding: 'I could name you half a dozen members of a rugby fifteen who would love the chance of a quiet chat with Thomas Walters Despain Esquire.'

Dando's quiet menace and the statue of 'The Lady of Justice' which capped the dome of the Old Bailey building were images that lingered in Quinn's mind, assuring him that Despain's ruthless crimes would not be unpunished. He remembered Charlie once saying: 'The past does not give up its secrets lightly. You have to bang on a few doors.' It seemed that the police had hammered on the right doors concerning the murder of their popular colleague.

The queue of mainly silent people found their way into No 1 Court which had a notice 'Poise the Cause in Justice's Equal Scales' above the doors. Quinn obtained a seat at the right of the Public Gallery which gave him a good view of the dock. After a few minutes there was a stir in the court as the Judge entered and took his seat. Mr Justice Hugh Beauchamp was an impressive figure wearing a scarlet robe trimmed with ermine. A tall, spare man, he had theatrical dark eyebrows, strongly marked features and wide grey eyes with the unblinking stare of an owl. Someone said, 'Put up the defendant' and there was another stir of excitement. A moment later Quinn saw Despain's blond head. He wore a grey flannel suit, white shirt and black tie. He stared round the court as if searching for someone, grimacing when he caught Quinn's eye. An old man sitting in front of Quinn commented, 'He's the spitting image of his father. Same arrogant look.'

Quinn did not agree with the old man's verdict since he thought Despain seemed much less arrogant than he had appeared in Paxos: he now had a prison pallor and looked as if he might already have learned a lesson or two. Despain lifted his jaw and squared his shoulders when he looked across at the Judge. Beauchamp regarded him with a cold stare.

A woman whispered, 'The trial starts with the arraignment of the accused. He's pleading not guilty so then the jury will be sworn.' Quinn moved restlessly about in his seat, uncertain whether to stay longer for he had seen what he wanted to see. He thought: I've done what I could and now the matter is in other hands. He decided that revenge was not sweet; it was just the unsatisfactory conclusion to a sad affair.

Quinn stood up and, lost in his thoughts, began to make his way out of the court. As he did so he felt someone clutch at his arm and looked down, expecting to see Daphne Vavasour, but instead he saw Anna Campaspe's luxuriant red hair and big brown eyes. She pulled a funny face and whispered, 'Enough?'

He nodded and said, 'Yes, enough.'

Anna followed him up the steps. Once the doors of the Court No 1 were closed behind them she said, 'I thought I might see Tamsin here, hoped I would.'

'Tamsin's locked up in Corfu, on a drug charge.'

'Poor girl.'

Quinn shrugged and said, 'Tamsin's been living in a dream world for years. Now she has had to face reality.'

'You're being hard on her.'

'Not at all. Despain had her hypnotised, and they committed crimes. But Despain's a villain and she's just foolish. I'd stand up for Tamsin any day. She saved my life in Paxos.'

'Saved your life?' Anna frowned and then raised her eyebrows.

'Yes, no doubt about that. But it's a long, long tale. Could take me hours to tell...' Quinn smiled. 'Perhaps days.'

'Well, I've plenty of time. I'm a free agent now.'

'Grand. Which way shall we go?'

'Any way, "if with me you'll fondly stray"?'

As they made their way along the empty corridor Quinn took Anna's left hand. She was wearing a brown dress with a gingerish coloured wool coat; in her right hand she held a brown fur hat. Quinn sighed and said, 'I'll be glad to get out of this bloody place. I want to forget all about Tom

250

Despain. I've been thinking of nothing else recently. I'll explain why some time, but not today.'

'Yes. Not today.'

As they stepped out of the Old Bailey building Quinn stood still for a moment and sniffed in the fresh air. Anna pulled on her hat and shivered in the east wind.

Quinn said, 'Right. So where to?'

'What about that house you can't afford?'

This Large Print Book for the Partially sighted, who cannot read normal print, is published under the auspices of

THE ULVERSCROFT FOUNDATION

THE ULVERSCROFT FOUNDATION

. . . we hope that you have enjoyed this Large Print Book. Please think for a moment about those people who have worse eyesight problems than you . . . and are unable to even read or enjoy Large Print, without great difficulty.

You can help them by sending a donation, large or small to:

The Ulverscroft Foundation, 1, The Green, Bradgate Road, Anstey, Leicestershire, LE7 7FU, England.

or request a copy of our brochure for more details.

The Foundation will use all your help to assist those people who are handicapped by various sight problems and need special attention.

Thank you very much for your help.